I0562806

These Tears for Hire

by

Lance Hawvermale

Copyright Notice
This is a work of fiction. Names, characters, places, and incidents are either the product of the author's imagination or are used fictitiously, and any resemblance to actual persons living or dead, business establishments, events, or locales, is entirely coincidental.

These Tears for Hire

COPYRIGHT © 2025 by Lance Hawvermale

All rights reserved. No part of this book may be used or reproduced in any manner whatsoever including the purpose of training artificial intelligence technologies in accordance with Article 4(3) of the Digital Single Market Directive 2019/790, The Wild Rose Press expressly reserves this work from the text and data mining exception. Only brief quotations embodied in critical articles or reviews may be allowed. Contact Information: info@thewildrosepress.com

Cover Art by *Lisa Dawn MacDonald*

The Wild Rose Press, Inc.
PO Box 708
Adams Basin, NY 14410-0708
Visit us at www.thewildrosepress.com

Publishing History
First Edition, 2025
Trade Paperback ISBN 978-1-5092-6144-4
Digital ISBN 978-1-5092-6145-1

Published in the United States of America

Dedication

For Charlie, whom I can never repay.

"Some things in life cannot be fixed. They can only be carried."

~ Megan Devine

Chapter One

In Which I Accept an Invitation

My husband was killed in the summer of '43 outside a French village with a name I can't pronounce. I used to blame General Patton for what happened. Then I switched to God, who is supposedly in charge. Finally I just settled on blaming the German who pulled the trigger. May he pray we never meet.

****

Monday, July 1, in the year of our lord Harry Truman 1946, arrives not with the tossing of the morning paper but with the cat walking across my face.

"*¡Vete!*" I scold him, using one of the few words I've managed to learn from the Cuban couple downstairs.

Satchel the cat, entirely unperturbed, commences grooming himself on the edge of the bed.

Roused before my time, I sigh and sit up. Blink a few times. Look around the gloom. I am what the radio programs would call A Lone Dame In A Bed Built for Two. Except I'm not alone. Satchel is the Humphrey Bogart to my Lauren Bacall.

Satchel, as if on cue, meows once, then settles in for his first of many siestas.

As for me, I cobble myself together one eyelash at a time and eventually throw open the curtains in the living

1

room. The back half of Kansas City has not changed in the night, with boys on bicycles and men in hats, with butchers in white, women in nylons, and the newspaper seller on the corner bellowing like a town crier of yore.

I open the window, a preemptive strike against what is predicted to be the hottest day of the year so far.

Nat Looper notices me immediately. "Hey, Mrs. Frisco!" he calls up from his usual post beside the wooden Indian at Corvin's Tobacco & Books. Nat can hold an honest job about as long as I can hold a high C. "You a bona fide attorney yet?"

"Give me another semester or two," I reply, leaning through the window.

"Take your time. Last thing this world needs is another lawyer." He laughs, expecting me to join him, so I do, but only a chuckle or two because law school is a pursuit I inherited from Jim, who dreamed of changing humanity for the better, one courtroom at a time.

He's been dead for three years now. They never found his body.

****

If you plan on visiting Kansas City, population a little over 125,000, I do not recommend any alley shortcut near Union Cemetery. The graveyard has been here since before the Civil War and fell into further disrepair when people suddenly had more important things to do after General Eisenhower led our boys into North Africa, beginning years of sacrifice for everyone. In many ways, our city is finally modernizing, now free of the privations of war. But this back lane is the alley that time forgot. If you sift through the pallets and generations of stacked debris, you'll find wagon wheels and probably the bones of some poor pioneer.

I catch my reflection in one of the few unbroken windows; my hickory-colored hair is darker in the glass, my brown eyes almost black. The twenty-nine-year-old looking back at me doesn't look a day past thirty-five. I emerge at the far end of the refuse, enter an unimpressive building, and cross the lobby. I stop in front of a wooden door reading SCHNEIDER LAW FIRM, but I know the brass name plate covers up a former inscription, SCHNEIDER AND FRISCO INVESTIGATIONS.

I step through this doorway, ghosts be damned.

****

I made bullets during the war. My part of "We can do it!" was eighteen months in a factory on the Missouri River, pressing slugs into brass casings. I made countless .30-06 cartridges for the BAR machine gun and so many .50-calibers for fighter aircraft that I sometimes see them lined up to infinity in my sleep. Other people count sheep.

"Morning, ma'am."

I glance at the custodian. "Hello, Kaz. Is he in?"

"Since sunrise."

"What? Why so early?"

He shrugs. "Big case, maybe? Or wife kicked him out?"

"Betty Schneider has never kicked anyone in her life."

"She wears nice shoes," Kaz says.

"Shoes that expensive should be a crime."

He does me a favor by not looking down at mine. I wear a pair of stacked-heel Kerrybrooke Oxfords that cost four dollars and change. They're brown and dependable and flattering in dim light.

"Have a good day, ma'am." He resumes the slow

waltz of his morning tasks.

"Hey, Kazuhiko."

The soft-spoken Japanese custodian looks back at me. "Yes?"

"Next time we meet, call me Vivian." I let myself into my husband's former office without a single knock.

****

Corky Schneider might be a practicing attorney these days, but he still decorates in a style I like to call Early Modern Private Investigator: chairs with the armrests worn smooth by nervous clients, a fan pushing hot air across the room, an ashtray on an open windowsill. A photo of Betty stands beside an autographed one of David Niven in military garb.

"Have a seat," Corky says.

For months after Jim's death, I refused to step through the doorway. Now I stop by at least twice a week, usually for Corky's help with my legal studies but sometimes just for the free coffee. I take the most comfortable chair and cross my legs. I'm wearing a plaid A-line skirt, and I pick at an errant thread I hadn't noticed until now.

"So how's your contract law class coming along?" he asks, lighting up a cigarette.

"You realize that no woman has ever climbed Mount Everest?"

"Come on, Viv. It can't be that hard."

"The mountain or the law degree?"

He exhales smoke that looks like a musical note. "You know I appreciate these social calls, and I consider myself a first-rate tutor when it comes to your homework, but since I have a client due in"—he tips his eyes toward his watch—"about twenty minutes, could we—"

"What kind of client?"

"Oh, you know, a wealthy and beautiful heiress with a Greek accent and a soft spot for first-year attorneys." He shakes his head. "You know I can't tell you anything about that."

"I know." I hold his gaze, and he doesn't look away. He's the only one who doesn't handle me gently; in the last three years, all of my friends have moved from *I am so sorry, you poor girl* to *Are you ever going to find your way in the world?* Corky is the only one who doesn't pity or misunderstand me. He and Jim enlisted together. Corky is thin where Jim was broad and sour where Jim was sweet. He came home with a lifelong hip problem and a Purple Heart. Then he completed their shared dream of transforming a lackluster detective career into what might become a respectable law firm.

"Viv?"

"Forget it. We have an assignment to interview a working attorney, but it's not due for a week. I'll come back."

"An interview, huh? You sure you wouldn't rather ask someone over at Covey and Bryant?"

"The lawyers at Covey and Bryant are more interested in their suits than in people."

Corky taps his cigarette three times. "You sure you're doing this for the right reasons?"

"The interview?"

"The career. The schooling to pass the bar exam. You know what I mean."

I *do* know what he means. "Can I come by tomorrow?"

"I'm free this afternoon."

"I have to work."

"Okay, sure. Tomorrow'll be dandy."

As I'm making for the door, he says, "You're still coming over for the Fourth? Betty refuses to have a backyard barbecue without you."

As I say, "Sure thing, Cork," I wonder which bachelor Betty's considering most eligible for me these days. When I visited to celebrate their anniversary a few months ago, it was a tennis coach from Rockhurst College. His name was Stan and he was excruciatingly nice. As I open the door, something occurs to me, and I look back. "Is everything all right?" I ask.

Corky pauses with the cigarette an inch from his lips. He didn't shave this morning. "Why would you ask that?"

"The dime novels call it extrasensory perception."

"Life isn't a dime novel, Viv."

"Tell me about it." I close the door softly behind me.

****

I may be the world's most mediocre law student by night, but by day I operate a telephone switchboard. I earn fifty cents an hour to pull this and push that, connecting calls between a spider's web of lines that seem to grow longer and more complex by the hour. Rural towns in Kansas and Missouri where old folks remember horses and buckboards are now linked to anywhere in the world—assuming I do my job correctly.

I walk the twenty minutes from Corky's office because I don't own a car—what single woman does?—but I'm certainly not the only pedestrian. The morning is beautiful. City workers hang colored bunting from street lamps. Shop clerks post Independence Day sales in their windows. Everyone waves at everyone else. When they stop to chat, they repeat a different verse of the same astonished song: Can you believe the war has been over for a whole nine months?

Trying to get into the spirit of things, I swing my purse with a bit more verve.

****

Nine hours later, my shift ending as uneventfully as it began, I get the usual ride from Ingrid and her husband, who kindly drop me off at the corner in front of Corvin's Tobacco & Books. The placard reads CLOSED— CAN'T WAIT TO SEE YOU TOMORROW. Rubbing at what might be an encroaching headache, I check the mail slot, find nothing, and manage to reach the second floor without entertaining a single intelligent thought. I have become a woman of habit, no longer needing to think to survive.

At last free of my shoes, I turn on the radio just in time for the evening replay of *The Amazing Mrs. Danberry* on CBS. While the title character trades quips with her co-stars, I warm up yesterday's liver loaf in the oven. Anything not made from wartime rations is fine cuisine. Satchel the cat spends time in my lap. We're both happy for the company. When the delightful Danberry gives way to the news report, I put up with it for three minutes before silencing the radio, soaking in the bath, and then finding my half of the bed just where I left it this morning. I should probably review my notes for the interview with Corky in the morning so as not to receive poor marks on the assignment, but I haven't the energy. There'll be time for that tomorrow, which I assume—wrongly, it turns out—will be no different than today.

Chapter Two

In Which I Encounter A Crime

I know precisely one magic trick. It goes like this:

I display a nickel between my thumb and forefinger, so that Nat Looper can see it clearly, even with his dimming vision. I close my left hand over it, apparently putting the coin into that hand but actually palming it in my right. After Jim passed, I taught myself to do this because *he* did it, and by mimicking him I somehow made the evenings a little less cold.

I reveal my empty hand. The coin has vanished.

Crouched in his dirty dungarees in front of the tobacco shop, Nat opens his eyes wide, smiling like a boy. "My gosh, Mrs. Frisco, you're a regular Blackstone!"

The coin reappears, and I drop it into his cup. "That's for luck."

"Mine or yours?"

My smile is faint and fey. With my briefcase in one hand and purse in the other, I begin my morning sojourn through the city.

****

Amelia Earhart disappeared exactly nine years ago to the day. Something about the human brain causes us always to recall where we were standing when disaster descends. For me, that pre-war July 2 in 1937 was spent at 3845 McGee Street, at the junior college where I studied whatever one studies at junior college—something about shorthand and home economics, probably. Mr. Killdaire interrupted study hall and said the unsayable. The great adventuress, the most famous woman in the world, had flown across the sea and vanished—like the coin in my hand. God had palmed her, and every young lady who aspired to be so brave was left wondering when He'd bring her back.

I emerge from the end of my favorite alley shortcut and see the police cars.

Two black-and-white Fords are parked in front of Corky's building. Traffic is stalled in both directions. I put my gloved hand up to shade my eyes from the sun. There are no other businesses in the building. The other office spaces are all vacant, having not yet found new occupants since the war. Perhaps someone broke in and relieved Corky of his autographed Dizzy Dean baseball.

Excessive curiosity, my pops used to say, will be the death of me.

I cross the street. I'm wearing my most dependable two-piece victory suit, the jacket and skirt in navy blue. The matching half-hat is pinned at an appropriate angle somewhere between jaunty and demure. A police sentry holds up a hand as I approach.

"Morning, ma'am."

"Officer." I glance over his shoulder. The building's door is propped open, which isn't unusual in the summer heat. Inside, silhouettes move with urgency. "What's going on?"

"Not at liberty to say."

"Was something stolen?"

"Maybe you didn't hear me the first time."

"My friend works here. I have an appointment."

"You should come back later, ma'am. Now is not a good time."

"I'm starting to get that idea." I realize, then, that nothing was stolen. This wasn't theft, but something worse. "Is Mr. Schneider okay?"

"Who?"

"The attorney with the ground-floor office." Of course he's okay. He's one of the liberators of France. He has shot men and been shot at in return. "Please. I need to know."

Apparently the officer is moved by the honesty in my voice, or he's one of those old-fashioned types who can't say no to a girl without pretense. "It wasn't him."

I nod slowly, not certain what to make of the phrase. *It wasn't him.* "Thank you."

I drift away, staying close to the building and hoping to make sense of what's transpiring within. A crowd has gathered. Someone from the paper has shown up, his press credentials met with unwelcome stares from the police. If the *Kansas City Star* is here, notepad in hand, then this evening's headline is happening right in front of me.

It wasn't him.

Translation: Corky Schneider is fine, but someone else in there is dead.

****

I wait for half an hour and at last he comes out.

Corky and Jim were friends for years before the war. Both revered the St. Louis Cardinals and recited batting averages at each other like lovers whispering sweet nothings across the room, but otherwise they were opposites. Corky wears his suits on the baggy side and his haircut a little too close to his scalp. He used to kid about the dark curls that sometimes touched my husband's ears in between barber visits.

I blink once, slowly, as I have learned so patiently to do. When I open my eyes, the memories are gone, replaced by Corky's worried look. "Hey, kid," he says. "Can you believe all this?"

"What's going on?"

Men in ties and shirtsleeves move in and out of the old art deco building. From inside, the reporter's camera flashes brightly.

Corky exhales and fishes out his cigarettes. Leaning heavily against a lamp post, he strikes a match and looks grim. "Apparently a homicide." He tips his head toward the tiny flame, then swipes out the match. "And I'm the lucky joe who found the body."

Of all the words in the English language, *homicide* is one that never loses its edge. It cuts through you. It leaves you standing there on a Kansas City sidewalk, questioning the stability of everything around you. I ask the only question worth asking: "Who is it?"

"The janitor."

"What?"

"The guy who mops the floors. The cleaner."

That makes no sense. I take a step back. "Kazuhiko?"

Corky blows out a funnel of smoke. "Yep."

"Kaz is dead?"

"Saw it with my own eyes. Head bashed in, by the looks of it."

"Someone murdered Kazuhiko?"

"For Christ's sake, Viv, you want me to spell it out for you? Yes, Mr. Kazuhiko Agawa is dead, killed by

11

numerous blunt impacts to the head, discovered and identified by yours truly as soon as I got to the building this morning."

"But…why?"

Corky rubs his face. He's always been a sweet guy, but he's seen men on the battlefield grated into chunks by machine-gun fire and friends face-up in shell holes half full of rainwater, so his patience for my disbelief is running out. "He's dead. Nobody knows why. Nothing is missing from any of the offices, and Agawa still has his wallet in his pocket. I don't have anything else to tell you. Except maybe go home and get some rest before your shift at the switchboard. I'll have Betty call you tonight and check on you."

"Wait." I stop him before he can leave me here alone with my disbelief.

He smokes and watches me.

"Did you…did you happen to hear what they're going to do?"

"What who's going to do?"

"The police."

"They'll investigate, I guess. But not much."

"What do you mean?"

"I mean this isn't exactly a high-priority case for them."

"A man is *dead*."

"Given these particular circumstances, there's only so much that can be done. That's just the way it is."

"Particular circumstances? What on earth are you talking about? Someone died in your building. You *found* him."

"I'm just saying that the police and prosecuting attorneys have…priorities. Do you understand what I'm trying to tell you here?"

"I don't believe I do, sir."

He rubs his eyes, cigarette pinched between his knuckles. Then he leans close enough that I can smell his aftershave. "It's like this. Number one, it's not like it's Babe Ruth lying dead in my lobby. It's a custodian. Number two, there isn't much in the way of physical evidence, from what I understand. And number three, he's a Jap and nobody cares."

"*I* care."

"Yeah, well, you and Jesus are the only members of that little club. These guys bombed our boys in Hawaii. And you heard what went on in the South Pacific with their POWs."

"Kaz wasn't involved in any of that."

"Try telling that to the cops."

"He baked corn pudding for me on my birthday."

Corky opens his mouth but thinks better of whatever war slang he was about to lay on me. He shakes his head. He looks tired and sad. "Go home, Vivian. I'll let you know if I hear anything, but I wouldn't sit by the telephone and wait if I were you."

And he leaves me there by the lamp post, all the answers just beyond my reach.

Chapter Three

In Which I Violate Policy

If you're like me, at work you always pretend that everything is fine.

Why, Mae, that dress is simply darling!

Be a dear, Ann, and share your compact with me. I left mine at home.

Of course I heard that new Benny Goodman number. Isn't it gorgeous?

And so on.

Fortunately, my job leaves room for conversation only during our lunchtime. Otherwise we are seated in a perfect line, facing a vast wall of telephonic equipment that we barely understand, connecting callers across western Missouri and eastern Kansas. The board in front of me features a tangle of color-coded cables. My job is to move a cable to its proper port. That's it. Repeat *ad nauseum* until the end of my shift. A caller in Olathe wants to speak to someone at the city library at 9th and Locust.

I say, "One moment, please," for the forty-seventh time that day, pull a cable, insert the cable, and then move on to a caller who needs a clerk at Zeff's Department Store on Southwest Boulevard—"preferably in the men's clothing department"—and so I say, "One moment, please," yet again and pull a different cable and shove it into a different hole.

During all of this, I think of Kazuhiko Agawa.

I barely knew him. Never once did I encounter him beyond the building where he worked. Kaz always said hello to me, and I said it back. We often chatted while I waited for Jim to finish whatever private eyes did behind closed doors to make themselves late for lunch with their wives. Kaz told me he learned English from a Jewish schoolteacher who lived next door when he was a boy. I confided in him my weaknesses—sugar and stray cats—and that made him laugh.

Who would ever want him dead?

No matter how many cables I connect or callers I serve, I fail to locate a reply to that. If he wasn't robbed and the building was otherwise undisturbed, his murder makes no sense. Wild theories occur to me. Kaz was a gambler in debt to the wrong people. Kaz had an affair with a dangerous man's wife. Kaz smuggled Nazi relics into rural Kansas towns.

The truth is probably more prosaic and primed by hate: He was Japanese.

American citizens of Japanese descent were held in camps of wire and wood until as recently as two years ago. They are the villains of our post-war world. A German, at least, looks like the rest of us. Asians are spat on in the street.

The clatter of work continues around me without slowing down. I am one of eight women working in a line, almost shoulder to shoulder, our hair neat on our heads, our voices anonymous and polite, our hands moving like pale quick birds along the board.

This is the moment when I decide to break the rules.

****

Pacing behind our row of swiveling metal chairs is the supervisor. Her name is Ms. Peele. In a past life, she was the headmistress at a colonial Puritan school. Of course that's hyperbole. She's not that bad at all, merely businesslike and firm. But the rest of us girls see her as the classroom marm with the ready ruler. A little chatter among us is fine. Ms. Peele simply says, "*Ladies,*" when that chatter threatens to become a conversation. In addition to her duties as taskmaster, she assists us with navigating the thick, spiral-bound book that contains indexed columns of numbers and telephone exchanges. Ms. Peele can locate a number more rapidly than any of us, even on her worst day. She is both sentry and servant.

In my mind, Corky says, *He's a Jap and nobody cares.*

I wait until Ms. Peele's constant steps have taken her to the farthest end of our line. Then I pull and push the next cable to route another call, except this call is for me. And for Kaz.

A voice answers midway through the first ring. "Sergeant Caruthers."

What am I doing?

What I'm doing is making sure I pay my respects. What I'm doing is finding the family of a slain custodian to let them know he was always kind to me. For whatever that's worth.

"Hello?"

"Yes, sir." My voice holds. "I'm told that this morning the police recovered the remains of Mr. Kazuhiko Agawa?"

"Sure, lady. All their names sound the same to me. But, yeah, Agawa, that's what we gave the press. You with the paper?"

"A family friend." I glance at Ms. Peele. She's on her way back.

"My condolences. Something I can do for you?"

"Do you happen to know how I can reach Mr. Agawa's wife?"

"I thought you said you were a family friend."

"We lost touch recently."

He exhales. From around him I can hear the clatter of the precinct. "Look, I don't have her name, and I probably couldn't give it to you if I did. But I *can* tell you that the cadaver's getting picked up by the Van Gording Funeral Home this evening. Maybe they can help you."

Ms. Peele stares at me as she closes the last few feet.

"Thanks." I pull the cable and grab the next call as Ms. Peele stops behind my shoulder.

"Everything all right, Vivian?" she asks.

"As rain, ma'am."

She stares at me for the next minute as I work. She can probably hear my heart beating from where she stands.

****

I have a telephone at home. Not everyone does. Mine is a pearly color, as sturdy as only Bakelite can be. Most models are black. Mine is the envy of my girlfriends, gentler on the eyes, a gift from the company president when word got around about my being a sudden widow.

Widow. Jesus Christ.

I close my eyes, my hand on the telephone that was given to me in hopes of helping alleviate my grief, so that I could connect with family or my in-laws or my little sister on the Jersey shore. Except I have no little sister or anyone else except Satchel, and he's a rotten conversationalist.

It's after seven in the evening when I open my eyes and dial the funeral home. My shift ended with Ms. Peele none the wiser. Maybe my aloneness is what makes me so desperate to contact Mrs. Agawa. Widows of a feather, flocking together. That almost makes me smile.

Using the number I found in the index at work, I call the mortician.

****

That night I have a dream about Harry Houdini.

I was seven years old when I saw him perform. My only remaining memory of his show was when he swallowed nearly a hundred sewing needles and then pulled them back up his throat, somehow all connected by a wet red thread. I was horrified and thrilled at the same time. In my dream, the late Mr. Houdini's string of needles has replaced my telephone cord, and my dream-self is afraid to answer when it rings.

I wake up in the darkness, displacing Satchel. The dream vanishes in a moment, as they sometimes do, leaving no lingering effects. My first thought is of the nice man at the Van Gording Funeral Home. He advised me to call back around lunchtime the next day, as the family had not yet Made Arrangements. He said it with capital letters.

I look at the clock but it's too dark to see anything. And it's hot. I'm covered by only a single sheet, but the hour is somewhere between July 2 and 3, the hottest stretch of days so far, and even at this time of night it's uncomfortably warm. Motion-picture stars and business moguls reportedly have air-coolers in their homes. I have a fan that squeaks when it moves.

I get up, adjust my old-maid's nightgown, and throw open the bedroom window.

The breeze is angled properly for once, cooling my face. And it must be a night for divine intervention, as the gentle wind is followed by the sound of a clarinet from across the street. I've never met the family who lives above the pastry shop, but they are all musicians. This one, playing "That Old Black Magic" to the lightless city streets, becomes my personal muse.

I whisper the lyrics and resign myself to not getting back to sleep.

Chapter Four

In Which I Meet the Airman

I interview Corky in the morning and use his office typewriter to complete my paper. It's eight double-spaced pages of academic mediocrity. I am a solid B-minus law student. I'm banking on the fact that my grade-point average won't be embossed on my diploma.

Before heading to my usual afternoon shift at the switchboard, I use Corky's telephone—nowhere near as lovely as mine—to dial Van Gording's again. The voice on the other end of the line is like that of an after-hours radio announcer. He is calm and consoling and pronounces every syllable as Noah Webster intended.

"Tomorrow afternoon at one o'clock," he tells me, "the family will hold a Shinto funeral in our own non-denominational chapel, followed immediately by a graveside service at the New Hope Cemetery here in Liberty."

I note these facts on my yellow legal pad. "What's a Shinto funeral?"

"I'm told it is a traditional Japanese service for the deceased."

"And you're located in Liberty?"

"That is correct."

I thank him and end the call. Liberty is about twenty miles from here, give or take. I don't own a car.

****

The closest thing I have to a living relative is my fake Uncle Charles. He's not my uncle by blood, but an old family friend. My parents passed years ago, and sometime shortly after that, Charles O'Brien became my surrogate uncle. He owns an automobile repair shop on Paseo Boulevard. He or his son Rudy sometimes usher me around on errands. On my salary, I can afford either a car or a roof over my head.

Taking advantage of Corky's kindness, I borrow his telephone again.

Charles answers the shop phone on the fourth ring, opening with his standard greeting that thanks the caller for contacting him and offering an assurance that his rates are the best on either side of the river.

"That's quite a mouthful, Uncle Charlie."

"Hey, that's my girl right there! How you been, darling?"

I tell him how I've been. I don't mention the bad parts.

"How're the studies going?"

"Slowly."

"Rome wasn't built in a day, right? And neither was Kansas City, for that matter." He laughs, a sound I don't hear often enough.

"May I ask a favor?"

"If it's you asking, then I assume you need a lift. You want me to swing by this afternoon after I close up?"

"Actually it's for tomorrow."

"Check your calendar," he says. "Tomorrow is a national holiday."

"I know."

"It's the biggest Fourth of July since 1776."

"*I know.*"

"Nobody in America is running errands tomorrow. All the stores'll be closed. Where could you possibly need to go?"

He's right. Everything will be closed. Except for a cemetery in Liberty, Missouri.

"Why don't you come over to Ted's with us?" Charles asks. "I'll be cooking all day, and my pork chops haven't killed any innocent bystanders since 1934."

"I appreciate the offer. I'll be visiting friends."

"Can't these friends of yours give you a ride?"

I sigh. Yes, Corky and Betty intend to deliver me to their place tomorrow night for the barbecue, but first of all, I have no intention of telling the two of them that I'm crashing Kaz's funeral, and second, they'll be busy getting ready for the party and won't have time to drive me twenty miles out of their way for a cause they don't understand. "I suppose I could—"

"Hold on a sec," Charles says. "Have you ever met my nephew?"

"I don't believe so."

"Name's Derek. He's on a month of shore leave from the Air Corps. He'll jump at the chance to show off his car to anyone who cares to look, holiday or not. Let me ask him if he can play chauffeur for a few hours."

"I can't impose on a total stranger."

"I told you he's my nephew, so enough with the stranger stuff. Derek is as much of an O'Brien as I am, though not quite as Irish. What time you want him to pick you up?"

We settle on a time. Derek O'Brien will escort me to the service. I'll pay him for his fuel and for his time—

and for waiting like a taxi driver while I say whatever I need to say to Kaz's wife. Maybe I simply need to tell her that her husband was always polite to me. Or maybe I need to make a speech.

"Oh, and Uncle Charlie?"

"Yeah, darling?"

"Tell your nephew to dress for a funeral."

****

On my walk to work that afternoon I find a piece of glass that looks like a diamond. I'm wearing cream-colored gloves that match my shoes, so I'm not terribly afraid of cutting myself when I pick it up and continue my journey, but it turns out to be quite smooth. It looks like a piece of a chandelier. At home is a hat box full of obscure objects found during my treks across the city. Perhaps all these years I've been picking up someone else's breadcrumbs, so it's my fault if they can't find their way back again.

Unlike yesterday, I conduct myself properly at the switchboard. In between calls, I ask myself why I'm so intent on attending a funeral to which I've not been invited. *He's a Jap and nobody cares.* I feel obligated. And somehow attached. If the psychologists are right and we're all just looking for closure, then maybe mine is waiting in a Liberty graveyard.

After work I go home and add the diamond to the box.

****

The next morning is the first Fourth of July since we won the war. By the time I slide from bed, the antics have started in the street. The family from above the pastry shop has arranged themselves as a quintet on the corner; a crowd has already formed. Even at this early hour, everyone enjoys a good Tommy Dorsey number accompanied by clarinet.

Pulling on a robe, I fetch the milk from the stoop and add a dash to my coffee. No one has really gotten back into the habit of real meals, not with wartime cupboards so fresh in everyone's minds. I end up with a bowl of oatmeal, made palatable with real sugar.

And now the question of a lifetime: What on earth do I wear?

I settle not on black but on what the Montgomery Ward catalog calls "midnight blue." It sounds almost romantic, which is not my intent. My intent is to approach a woman I've never met and say nice things about her husband that she won't remember by this evening. Once that's done, I'll come back, change into something airy and patriotic, and play nice at the Schneider soiree this evening.

Here I am at the mirror. I wear my hair with a full-rolled bottom, keeping it off my neck in the heat. My earrings are small faux pearls. My brown eyes have always seemed a little too wide to me, like a woman surprised all the time.

Maybe that's true. But I'm not surprised by the knock on the door. My carriage driver is right on time.

****

Derek O'Brien should be holding a football. He looks like one of those chaps from Yale, ready to pose for a sports photographer, a halfback fending off a tackler. He's taller than I expected him to be.

"Mrs. Frisco?"

"Mr. O'Brien."

And with that simple exchange of names, we trade passports for wherever our expedition may lead. By the time we reach the sidewalk in front of my building, we're skirt-deep in a disagreement.

"…but every time I turn on the radio," he's saying, "all I hear about are the trials at Nuremberg."

"You don't think prosecting war criminals is important?"

"I'm an officer in the Army Air Corps. Of course it's important."

"Then what are you saying?"

"I'm saying the news agencies may be overlooking a lot of important issues here at home in favor of waiting with bated breath to report that a bunch of Nazis are to be hanged."

I stop there in the morning sun and appraise him. I've known him for approximately two and a half minutes. His blond hair is short and smooth. He wears black trousers, a black tie with a silver tie bar, and a shirt as white as sailcloth. Yes, definitely a football player from Yale.

"That look on your face says I already owe you an apology," he says.

"I do admit that hangings aren't high on my list of conversation topics."

He winces. "Forgive me."

"Think nothing of it."

"I'm notoriously bad at meeting people. I'm much better in the air than on the ground."

"Perhaps you should have picked me up in a plane."

And then he smiles. "I'll keep that in mind. As it turns out, I brought the next best thing." He motions toward the car.

Sitting at the curb is a black convertible with a red leather interior and whitewall tires. A pair of exhaust pipes snarl from either side of the motor, like chrome fangs.

Though Derek O'Brien is probably almost thirty years old, strong and confident in his polished shoes, he is like every fully grown man I've ever met—a jubilant boy when in the presence of a low-slung automobile. So I do him a favor and ask for details. "What is it?"

"It's a 1937 Cord. The supercharged Phaeton model."

"And the engine?"

"You're seriously interested in that?"

"Pretend that I am."

He grins. "She's holding a Stromberg duplex carb-fed 289 cubic-inch V8, capable of 170 horsepower. Some folks think it's the perfect combination of power and prestige."

I turn from this sphinx of a car to look at him. "What important issues here at home?"

"I'm sorry?"

"You said that instead of reports from Nuremberg, we should be worrying about matters here at home. Like what?"

"Oh, I don't know. Like new bridges and roads."

"I didn't realize those were problems."

"When you see things from the sky, they look a lot different."

"I suppose they do." Across the street, the quintet has commenced an a cappella version of "Remember Pearl Harbor."

"May I get your door?" he asks.

I only nod. Suddenly I want to skip several hours ahead to this evening at the Schneider backyard, where the only things that matter are Betty's blue moon cocktails and Corky's bad Gene Autry impersonations.

The car door is hinged at the rear. It opens like the blade of a knife.

I slide inside, and the knife closes.

Chapter Five

In Which I am Given an Envelope

We keep the top up on the way to Liberty. The car's interior smells of the conditioner rubbed into the leather. Derek wears driving gloves with little holes above every knuckle—an affectation. I've never ridden in a convertible. Given our destination, the breeze in our hair would have been a violation. We should be speaking of somber topics, of heavy things, or at least the sanitized version of those things discussed by two people who only just met. But instead, we're talking about my cat.

"His name is Satchel, like a suitcase?" Derek asks. "A backpack? That sort of thing?"

"No. Like the pitcher."

His fingers are light on the Cord's steering wheel. He glances over. "I don't follow."

"Do you keep up with baseball?"

"As much as any other fellow in the military. Someone is always reading off the box scores."

"Satchel Paige pitches for the Kansas City Monarchs."

"Ah, the Negro League." He nods.

"He'll get called up soon enough."

"And pitch against DiMaggio? Your cat might have better odds."

From there, grasping for things to say to each other,

we move through an index of the usual topics: the searing temperatures, the return of quality motion pictures to the cinemas, and the currently popular radio shows. We also talk about work. Mine feels prosaic against his.

"How long have you been in the Air Corps?" I ask.

"Six years and counting. I thought I'd make a career of it, but the Boeing Airplane Company is paying foolish amounts of money for test pilots, so I'm considering betraying old Uncle Sam, so to speak, instead of re-upping."

"Did you see much action?"

He shrugs. "Here and there."

I sense there's more to it. His *here and there* means *yes, a lot of it*.

"Bombers?"

"Those lumbering whales?" He shakes his head. "No, thank you. I fly the P-51 Mustang."

Almost immediately I say, "The Mustang is fitted with six 50-caliber Browning machine guns."

Derek snaps his head at me as he drives. "How do you possibly know that?"

"I manufactured high-caliber ammunition during the war. You might have shot at a German pilot with bullets loaded by my own hand."

"I'll be damned."

Neither of us knows what to say after that. This moment on the sun-splashed road, moving at what seems like a comet's pace, takes the place of conversation. During the war, everyone abided by a speed cap of 35 miles an hour to save on rubber and gasoline. Now that limit is gone.

* * * *

Though I have no evidence, I'm mostly certain this

is the only funeral in the nation being held on Independence Day. I stand in the back corner of a supernaturally bland chapel. Nothing in this sanctuary could offend any particular denomination; it is as if the Bureau of Statistics decided to design a church.

Having donned a black suit coat, Derek stands nearby. He whispers: "What's going on?"

I already gave him the basics of why I'm here. When I told him that I was Kazuhiko's friend, I exaggerated. "Shinto funeral rites," I reply.

A Japanese man in a white robe and peaked black headdress stands at the front of the room, near Kaz's carefully arranged body. From where I stand, I can't quite see his gentle, familiar face. Most of him is covered by an ivory-colored cerecloth. The Shinto priest has the look of a statesman, worn but dignified, and his voice is the only sound other than the near-quiet waving of the fan in the hands of one of the attendees. Eight other people are here, all of them Japanese. I can't understand the priest's words, but I suspect he's giving the same line as any other minister at times like these: *lived a life of reward, beloved by his family, going to a better place.* The sameness of these universal sentiments makes them difficult to believe.

The ritual continues. The movements are arcane. I know nothing of the Shinto faith, what god they worship, what value they place on kindness or Sunday mornings. I hold very still.

I can see only the backs of those in front of me, but I suddenly realize which one is Kaz's widow. She stands directly in front of me, her black hair pinned high and mostly covered by a veil. I recognize her because she is the only one not moving, not swaying slightly, not shifting from one foot to the other, not subtly scratching an itch. She is frozen in this moment, trapped in the amber of loss. I know her posture because, not long ago, it was my own.

Derek O'Brien, to his credit, is a silent, physical presence and nothing more.

With a word from the priest, several of the men step forward. They wear suits that are dated, inexpensive, ill-fitting. They have lived in American-built concentration camps until only recently. They have done more sorrowful things than this. Each takes up an edge of the bindings around Kaz's body, and at a nod from the priest, they lift as one, bearing him without effort to the waiting casket.

Now I see his face. He looks no different than when I saw him two days ago. The morticians here at Van Gording's have made the crater in his skull disappear.

I believe Kaz was murdered because he was Japanese. I believe he was murdered because of that cross-section of hatred called xenophobia. Or because, like the song says, we remember Pearl Harbor. I say none of this to his family.

His wife speaks little English. Her son Hiroto explains this briefly to me in a hushed tone after the casket has made its way outside. When I introduce myself, he relays this to his mother, Aika, who gives me one of those smiles that we manufacture purely out of will.

Hiroto translates her reply: "She says that she knows your name. You are the detective."

"Uh, no, not exactly…"

"Frisco is the name from the office where my father worked, yes?"

"Well, yes. I mean, it used to be. That wasn't me." I shake my head. "It doesn't matter. I want to tell her that Kazuhiko was a good man. He was always very polite to me. She has my deepest sympathies for her loss." Once out of my mouth, the words sound like things I plagiarized from a sympathy card.

Hiroto gives her my message, and then she does something I didn't expect: she bows.

I've never been bowed to or bowed to anyone in return. Derek gives me an almost imperceptible nod, and I execute the best one I can muster.

"Thank you," Aika says in English. Her face is gentle, her eyes red. The lines around her mouth grant her esteem, a lovely maturity that seems elusive to most of us as we age. She is barely five feet tall.

"You're welcome." I look at Hiroto. "Would it be okay if I came to the graveside service?"

"Of course." He nods his head deeply.

They move away from me almost without sound.

"You okay?" Derek asks a moment later.

"The jury's still out." I watch the family. They're bent close together, whispering. Hiroto glances back at me.

"I think they're talking about you," Derek says.

"Maybe I shouldn't have come."

"Actually, I would guess they're honored by your presence."

"I should have said something less generic."

"You were fine."

"Nothing is fine about any of this."

"Do the police have any leads?"

"I'm told that the police aren't overly interested in what happened."

Derek rubs his smooth jawline but says nothing more.

Hiroto bows to his mother and moves brisky through the big double doors, sunlight streaming briefly inside. Then the doors softly close, cutting off the summer light.

****

Most dead people in Japan are cremated. I remember reading that somewhere when reports started coming in about daily life inside the concentration camps in California. But Kaz's family, like many, is half Americanized by now, their practices a blend of old-world tradition and U.S. custom. So the soft-spoken custodian who supported his family by cleaning office toilets will be put into the ground with the Christians.

I stand in the sun at the cemetery. It's the Fourth of July. A few hours from now, every small-town sky will light up. Today we celebrate as a union. Less than one year ago, we dropped a pair of atomic bombs and killed a quarter of a million people who looked like the Agawa family.

Men in suits lower the simple box into the ground. The Shinto priest is now attended by a young woman in a black kimono. He talks. She taps a bamboo drum. Derek and I are the only two white faces—other than the pair of cemetery workers who stand by the gate, smoking and waiting with their spades. Occasionally Derek glances at me, as if I might need to be steadied. Maybe he assumes I'm having flashbacks to the last memorial service I attended. I want to tell him I've visited that one enough in my dreams that I'm not tempted to return today.

And then it's over.

The family members take their last looks. They grip

each other's hands and elbows. They disperse.

I turn away, blinking a few times, touching the corner of my eye with a gloved hand.

Derek puts his hands in the pocket of his trousers. "You want to know what my Uncle Chuck told me about you?"

"I don't know. Do I?"

"He said that you remind him of a line from the Irish poet Oscar Wilde."

"Something irreverent, I'm assuming."

"Not at all. Chuck was in one of his serious moments. He said that dreamers like you can find your way forward only by moonlight, and your punishment is that you see the dawn before the rest of the world."

I look up at him. A lot goes through my mind. First, I never knew that Charlie O'Brien ever had a poetic thought in his head, and second, his nephew Derek is turning out to be—

"Pardon, ma'am?"

I turn to see Hiroto Agawa bow. When he straightens, I note the pain in his face. He's younger than me by at least ten years, his thin spectacles forming little silver circles around his eyes.

"May I speak?" he asks.

"Yes, of course."

"On behalf of my family, and at the request of my mother, I would like to offer you an arrangement."

"An arrangement? I don't understand."

He extends an envelope to me. "Please."

I don't know why I hesitate. Something about the moment feels perilous.

Hiroto's eyes move from me to the envelope and back again. His hand trembles.

Slowly I accept the offering. The envelope feels thick, as if several pieces of paper are folded inside.

"Please do us the honor," he says, "of learning who murdered my father."

"I…" Something's wrong. Hiroto and Aika have misunderstood. It's not my name on the office door. I need to find the correct words to explain without making the situation any sadder than it already is.

But then Hiroto says, "You have my gratitude," and he gives a nod and walks away.

I look down at my hand. Seconds pass.

After a while, Derek says, "Are you going to open it?"

Chapter Six

In Which I Learn of the Second Building

I was fifteen when I kissed my first boy. It was 1932. These days they're calling it the Great Depression. Back then it was simply life, and it went on just fine for me, mainly because my sweetheart's nickname was Ace.

You can do no wrong with a handle like that. If someone calls you Ace and the name sticks, it means you're really good at something. Maybe billiards or sharpshooting or throwing a ball. Ace Norris scored perfectly on nearly every assignment in school. His family moved away the season after our summer romance. I hear he graduated a year early and went on to West Point. Whatever happened to him, I'll probably never know.

"So what are you going to do?" Derek asks, driving us back to KC.

I stare from the passenger's window at the bright afternoon, the envelope between my knees. Ace told me something one night while we were necking on his parents' porch. He said, "The best people in the world are the ones who don't let go."

All I wanted at that point was to keep on running my hands through his hair. "What do you mean?"

"If something's not right, they try to fix it, even when everyone else has forgotten."

I assumed he was talking about his father or someone.

"That's how you are, Viv." He looked at me in the semidarkness from inches away. "And I think that's really swell."

I look over at Derek. "Say again?"

He flicks his eyes toward my lap. "Are you going to keep it?"

I look down. The envelope is filled with money. It's a random assortment of bills totaling 965 dollars. "This is probably every bit of savings they have."

"And they've given it to you."

"I tried to give it back. You saw me."

"What I saw was a business transaction."

"Hardly. The Agawas think I'm an investigator because they heard the name Frisco and assumed that I was a part of my husband's firm from years ago, which I never was. Why didn't you help me explain?"

"Don't drag me into this. I just met you a few hours ago."

"Kaz's death is not something I can resolve."

"So you'll keep their money and do nothing?"

The heat rises in my neck. "I'm a switchboard operator, for God's sake."

"Fair enough. I suppose you can use the money to hire an actual detective."

The suggestion has merit. We ride for a mile in silence, and the plan gains traction in my mind. I'll ask Corky to point me toward a possible private eye who's willing to take the case.

From somewhere in the past, Ace raises a knowing eyebrow.

****

I talk Derek into escorting me to the Schneider barbecue that evening. He admits his plans consisted of little more than drinking a few beers in a lawn chair at Charlie's and watching the local kids toss firecrackers at each other.

"Most of my friends are back on base or home with their families," he says.

"Sorry if I came across as being too forward. Don't feel like you have to come."

"Not at all. It sounds like the best offer I'm going to get."

"I tend to take advantage of people with cars."

"If there's free food and drink involved, I'm game. Besides, what could be more patriotic than a neighborly cookout and a game of horseshoes? I'll change clothes and pick you up in plenty of time. Maybe we'll put the top down on the Cord."

I'm off work today. The newer girls have been assigned the holiday shift. I've worked there since the surrender of the Axis powers, which makes my employment sound much more dramatic than it actually is. Determined not to labor there until spinsterhood, I'm attending law school at the University of Missouri's campus on Holmes Street. Our college's kangaroo mascot was drawn by a cartoonist who has since found fame in the creation of an increasingly popular mouse.

And so I opt for a bit of collegiate flair, adding a blue-and-gold scarf to a breezy blouse and matching it to a prairie-style skirt that hopefully doesn't make me look too much like a cast member from *Oklahoma!*

I told Kaz, *Next time we meet, call me Vivian.*

The next time I met him, he was draped in white and about to be put into a box.

I turn away from the mirror. My sadness, it seems, is slowly being replaced by anger.

I lean out my apartment window, hopeful for air. A parade happened while I was in Liberty, and now the neighborhood boys are earning a nickel each for scampering about with burlap bags for all the little pieces of red, white, and blue trash in the street.

When one of them looks up and waves, I give him a smile that doesn't reach my heart.

****

Derek wears tan linen trousers and white shoes that match his short-sleeved white shirt, its leather buttons revealing that it was made during the war when metal was scarce. His hair is slightly out of place, meaning the fabric roof has been retracted on the Cord. My doorway frames him in a way that seems imaginary; men do not stand in my doorway like that.

"Betty's going to talk, you know," I tell him as I gather my purse.

"Come again?"

"About the fact you're driving me to the party."

"Ah."

"I apologize in advance if she interrogates you."

"I've survived tighter scrapes."

"She's a busybody, but she's my friend."

"If you want, I could…just wait in the car."

"Don't be silly. I only wanted to warn you that you might find yourself the object of old wives and their tales."

"Wouldn't be the first time," he says, and motions for me to go ahead.

I step out, lock my apartment door, and think about the packet of money I hid beneath the bed.

****

Parties such as these are like solar systems. The genders form their own planets—women here, men over there—and we all revolve around the food. The conversations are as different as alien atmospheres.

"…and I told her we *all* look that way in the morning, sugar," Betty says.

We laugh. I join in. We all feel good. How can we not? We are four middle-class white mademoiselles with liquor in our glasses and the Andrews Sisters on the record player.

Darby Skinner works at an ad agency; her husband writes marketing copy and she line-edits him. "When Gene and I were dating, he never once saw me before eleven in the morning. That was my rule."

"A lady does need time to process herself," Katrina agrees, her cigarette inserted into one of those long holders that make her look European.

"Gene, though, spends no more than fifteen seconds in front of the mirror before he's ready to go. A little bit of aftershave and he thinks he's a movie star."

"Same with Corky," Betty says. "I once suggested that he try my facial moisturizer, and you'd have thought I asked him to light his skin on fire."

Katrina exhales smoke. "Is this where I'm supposed to say 'boys will be boys'?"

"Men," Darby says, "you can't live with them—"

We all say it together: "And you can't just drown them."

Smiles all around. Cocktail glasses touch.

Such are the signposts of any successful social event. Everyone giggles lightly, no one rants about politics, and everybody gossips about anyone who didn't show up.

Suddenly Betty is guiding me away by the elbow on the pretense of refilling our glasses. "So...who is this Derek person?"

"I suppose the question was inevitable."

"Indeed." We stop by the wooden fence at the back of the yard, upwind from the chicken on the grill. Betty holds her glass in front of her face and stares at me over the rim. She has done her hair in such a way that each curl looks placed by a person in charge of magazine ads. "Before you say anything, Vivian, I want to admit that he is absolutely smashing and every one of us here is, quite frankly, stunned to see you with him."

"I'm not *with* him."

"He looks like Errol Flynn. Of course you're with him."

"I just met him this morning."

"Well, then clearly your morning was much more interesting than mine." She sips the last of her drink. "Either way, hon, I'm glad you brought someone." Her smile is genuine. "I worry about you sometimes, you know."

I catch myself before I say *I'm fine*, instead opting for, "Do you mind if I steal your husband for a minute?"

"Are we trading? Normally I wouldn't be tempted, but did you say Mr. O'Brien flies fighter planes?"

"It's about work. Law stuff."

She sighs. "Of course it is. You're going to have to lighten up one of these days. That's in the women's handbook, page twelve, paragraph four. Thou shalt not live alone with a cat until menopause."

A few minutes later, I'm standing on the back porch with Corky, who holds a beer in one hand and a spatula in the other. The handle of the spatula is in the shape of the Statue of Liberty. Corky can tell I'm about to break party protocol and talk about our day jobs, so he braces himself with a long pull from his bottle. "All right, lay it on me. But keep in mind that our dinner is on the coals, and I don't trust Patterson not to burn it while I'm away."

Maybe there was a time in my life when I would have chosen a soft angle for my approach, but now I simply say, "This is about Kazuhiko Agawa."

"Ah, hell…" He shakes his head at me and takes a step off the porch.

"Corky, please."

"Please what?"

"Don't you want to know who did that to him? And why?"

"I already know the *why*, Vivian. And so do you. Americans hate the Japanese. And with good reason. Take a quick poll at this party and see where we stand. Yes, I'm an upstanding and curious citizen, and I would love seeing his killer get justice, et cetera. But is there a damn thing I can do to help make that happen? Absolutely not."

"I'm not asking for your help, at least not that directly."

"Then what, huh? What are we doing here?"

"Just give me the name of an investigator."

"Give you the name…" He grins without mirth and swallows the last bit from his bottle. "Okay, now I understand what you want to do. I get it. I'm no longer in the private eye business, so you want me to point out someone who is, someone foolish or desperate enough to take the case. Am I right?"

Derek approaches. I guess he sees something in my

face.

"Surely someone can find some answers," I say. It sounds weak, even to me.

"Look, this isn't Chicago. We don't have a pressing need for detectives on these streets. I know a couple of cops who do it on the side for extra cash, but that's mainly cheating husbands and the occasional insurance fraud."

"Fine. It's a lost cause. I get it. But if this was before the war and you were going to look into it, back when you and Jim were doing this kind of thing, where would you start?"

This line of questioning seems to suit him. He moves from the defensive to the contemplative. "Well"—he taps his bottle against his leg—"I suppose I'd set aside my assumption that Agawa was killed because he was a Jap and interview the folks who knew him. First, that would be his family, and second, that would be the offices he cleaned."

"There aren't any other active offices, not since before the war. No one is there but you."

"Sure, but the guy cleaned our building in the morning and another one in the afternoon."

"He did?"

"You think he could make ends meet otherwise?

"What other building?"

"I think he said it was somewhere on Benton Street. All I know is that one of the businesses there is a boxing gym, on account of Agawa saying he got to watch the fights for free. So that's what I would do, Viv, if I were still foolish enough to try and gumshoe in this town. Now I gotta get back to my roasted chicken before it dies a fiery death. Good luck. And don't do anything dumb."

He walks away. The sun drops lower toward the horizon. In the distance, fireworks sound like the Browning machine guns they used to test behind the factory where I worked.

Derek clears his throat.

"Yes?"

"May I make an observation?" he asks.

"Go ahead."

"I only just met you, yet something tells me that you're making plans to visit this mysterious building on Benton Street."

"I only just met *you*, yet something tells me that you're itching to come along."

And then Derek does something that saves the day. He throws back his head and laughs.

Chapter Seven

In Which I Set the Game Afoot

My Fourth of July ends with Nat Looper beside the wooden Apache chief. Nat wears a paperboard hat in the style of Uncle Sam. Someone has put a matching hat on the statue. The sky is dark. I hold my shoes in my hand. But before I can go upstairs to my apartment, Nat says, "God spoke to me today, Mrs. Frisco."

"Is that so? I'm afraid to ask."

"What, you don't think the Almighty speaks to washed-up old fools?"

"Actually washed-up old fools are probably His favorite people."

"Thank you." He rubs his chapped face. "God told me to watch out for you."

That isn't what I was expecting.

"He said it just like that," Nat continues, gesturing vaguely. " 'Look out for her, Nathaniel J. Looper.' "

"I'll be okay. But I appreciate the concern from both of you."

Nat starts to ramble about memories of Sunday school when he was a boy, and I leave him to his monologue, advancing up the stairs to my apartment above the lovely couple who speak Spanish to each other, their words sometimes gliding up to my window and reminding me of places I've never been.

****

Morning arrives on feline feet. As is often the case, Satchel calls reveille well before he should. All the way to the kitchen, he reminds me that we're down to our last two cans of cat food; a trip to the market is in order. I add that to my list of things to do, right after I ask around about a murderer.

My shift at the telephone exchange begins at three this afternoon, giving me several hours to locate the building with the boxing gym and interview whomever I find. After eating a quick breakfast and getting dressed, I extract two hundred dollars from the envelope the Agawa family gave me and put it in my purse. That done, I slide *Gone with the Wind* from my modest bookshelf, open it at random, and stash the remainder of the money somewhere in the middle of Scarlett O'Hara leasing prison convicts to work her mills. I'm sure there's a lesson in that.

Footsteps on the stairs indicate that Derek is as punctual as only pilots can be.

One last glance in the mirror—the woman looking back seems neither extraordinary nor particularly well equipped for the task at hand, but her complexion is nice. None of that matters. I'm not the person who owes the debt to Kaz, but it looks like I'm the one who will see that it's collected. I don't want the job. But I understand it's now mine. Once you pull out the sword, it can't go back in the stone.

****

The Cord's engine rumbles to life like something born in a cave.

"Do you know how to get to Benton?" I ask as Derek dons a pair of sunglasses with silver frames.

"I was hoping you could serve as navigator," he says.

"You're not familiar with the city?"

"I visit Uncle Chuck twice a year. Otherwise, no."

"Where's home?"

"Wherever the Air Corps sends me."

"So you're a vagabond?"

"Oh, it's not so bad. I don't have a mortgage payment or a lawn in need of clipping."

"Lucky for me, you *do* have a car." I give him directions and glance up at the sky. The convertible's top has been stowed away. The morning wind gathers strength. I extend my arm and gather some air in my fist.

Using the address I found for Budanov's Boxing Club, we arrive at a three-story brick building twenty years past its prime. A single concrete cherub hangs halfway up the front façade, two jagged gaps beside him indicating that other angels broke apart and left him alone.

Derek shuts off the engine.

For a moment, I do nothing. My investigative skills go no further than what I overheard Jim discuss at our tiny dining table and what I've read in Ellery Queen novels. And suddenly the grief returns, unapologetically dark. My eyelids close without my consent. My breath stops moving up and down my throat. The familiar timelessness of sorrow returns and expands and asks if I would like it to pull me apart yet again; it's been so long.

"Mrs. Frisco?"

I still have that same dining room table. On one edge is a small mark—a burn. Jim's cigarette slipped from the ashtray when he stood up suddenly, gathered me against him, and pulled me to the floor.

"Hey."

I open my eyes. Derek's hand rests lightly on my shoulder. "Forgive me for saying so, but—"

"But I look like shit?"

"Well, I was going to say you look *pale,* but…"

"Come on." I swing open the stupid backwards car door and slam it shut behind me.

****

The guy in the red trunks needs to practice his footwork. Even I can see that. Derek and I walk around the ring, with its aging canvas and sagging ropes, while the man in the blue trunks lands three out of five punches on his mostly sedentary target. The windows are open to vent some of the heat and sweat-stink, so birds have invited themselves inside to roost on the exercise equipment. Over in the corner, beneath a single bare bulb, a trainer yells at a black boxer that he'll never be the next Joe Louis if he doesn't hit that bag like he means it.

"I trust you have a strategy here?" Derek asks as we approach an office with its windows covered in placards advertising past fights. "Some kind of…plan of attack?"

"I'm not attacking anyone."

"Fair enough."

"But I have some questions in mind, yes."

"And my role is to intimidate the witness?"

I glance at him to see if he's serious. He isn't.

The office is filled with exactly what I expected: a few trophies, photographs pinned to the wall, newspaper clippings stuck to a corkboard. There's also a French bulldog sprawled in front of the desk, giving us an acknowledging yawn as I stop at the doorway and knock twice on the jamb.

"Yeah, I'm here." The man behind the cluttered desk wears a newsboy hat, his shirtsleeves rolled to his elbows. He looks at us from across an open ledger, a fountain pen in his left hand. "Something I can do for you folks?"

I introduce myself. Derek does the same. Then I ask for Mr. Budanov.

The man shakes his head. "Yuri Budanov left to help his motherland on the Eastern Front in the middle of the war. His last contact was a telegram to his wife in November two years back."

"I see. And you are…the new owner?"

"More like the unofficial manager on behalf of Mrs. Budanov. I'm Vic Penilo. Yuri was my boss."

"A pleasure to meet you."

"Likewise. Pardon my saying so, but you don't exactly look like our usual clientele, so I assume you're not here for lessons in the sweet science."

"The sweet science?"

Derek says, "He means prizefighting."

"I do indeed," Vic confirms. "You a fight fan, sir?"

"Depends on the fighters."

"Well said. So"—he leans back in his chair—"what can I for the two of you?"

This is my cue. Except my carefully prepared soliloquy suddenly escapes me.

The French bulldog rolls over on its side and exhales dramatically.

Derek gives me a look. "Mrs. Frisco?"

"Right. Sorry." I gather myself. "We're not here regarding Mr. Budanov or boxing at all. Rather, I'd like to talk about a man named Kazuhiko Agawa."

"Agawa?"

"I believe he might serve as your custodian…?"

"Sure, I know who you're talking about. Agawa spends a lot of time here. He's friendly with the fighters. Attends a lot of bouts. Seems like a decent guy. He do something wrong?"

I have no better way of framing it than to say, "Mr. Agawa has passed away."

Penilo leans forward, his chair creaking. "You serious? How?"

Derek saves me from having to say it: "He was murdered."

Penilo removes his cap. He blinks a few times.

I plunge ahead. "We're hoping you can help us answer a few questions that might aid the police in their investigation."

"Uh, yeah, of course." He drops his cap onto the desk and rubs a hand across his closely cropped hair. "Who did it?"

"We don't know."

"Damn, I just saw the guy. I mean, he was just here with his broom, doing his thing, chatting up the fighters…you two with the cops?"

"Friends of the family. Do you think you can help us?"

"I'll do everything I can. Wow." He takes a pack of cigarettes from his desk drawer and lights one, extinguishing the match in an ashtray made from what looks like the base of a 40-millimeter M1 shell casing; I know my armaments, having filled so many.

"Kazuhiko was the custodian here?" I ask.

"For a while now, yeah. Didn't know anything about the fight scene when he got here but became a real fan."

"How so?"

"Well, we didn't exactly pay him a lot, so we let him into all the bouts on a *gratis* basis. He made friends with a lot of the guys who train here. Backed up his favorites with wagers on Saturday nights. You really have no idea who might have killed him?"

"Not yet."

"He get shot or stabbed or something?"

"More or less. Did you say he was a gambler?"

"Who isn't? Making odds on pugilists is a pastime as old as the sport itself. I imagine when two cavemen had the first fistfight, there was at least one fella betting a wolf pelt on who was going to win."

I start to speculate on things I don't really understand, like bookmaking and unpaid markers. Am I already out of my depth? I just got started. "So…Kazuhiko had some outstanding loans?"

"Come again?"

"Gambling debt. I assume he accumulated a certain amount."

Penilo snorts. "Actually, it's the exact opposite of that."

"What do you mean?"

"I mean I wish I had his luck." Penilo exhales a funnel of smoke. "Agawa won almost every boxing bet he placed."

The French bulldog snores lightly at my feet. I've accepted Vic Penilo's offer and taken a seat, Derek in a chair beside me. Our conversation is punctuated by the sounds of punches from the adjacent gym.

"…but Agawa was friendly with everybody and never uttered a cross word," Penilo is saying, "so the guys here didn't make a big deal of him being Japanese."

"Everyone liked him?"

"Or ignored him, yeah. But he really took a shine to some of the fighters, young guys who barely knew a boxing glove from a frying pan when they got here. One or two of them he even helped out."

"Helped out?" Should I be writing this down? I wonder if I'm doing it right. Maybe I should've brought a notebook. "How so?"

"Like with their membership fees. We ain't running a charity here, Mrs. Frisco. If I don't pay the bills, Mrs. Budanov is going to be finding somebody else to run the place. Most of the fellas who sign on think they're going to be the second coming of Jack Dempsey, but two months later they lose interest. Some, though, have real potential but not enough money. Agawa was known to take his winnings and invest in that kind of fighter."

"And he often won when he bet on a match?"

"I guess he had a nose for it. He got to know the fighters while he was pushing his mop around. He saw them train every day. That's a pretty good way to hedge your bets."

"Did you ever find it...*odd* that he won so frequently?"

"Nah. Had there been serious money at stake, I would've been suspicious that he had some kind of fix on the fight. But Agawa rarely put more than fifty bucks down at a time, and usually it was only ten or twenty. Hell, sometimes only five. He was a janitor, not some high-roller."

Derek crosses his legs. "You say he used his money to invest in particular boxers?"

"That's right."

"Which ones?"

It's a good question. I look from Derek to Penilo,

who takes a drag and says, "A few dropped out or moved on to something else, like I was saying they do. But there are two that Agawa really took a shine to, and they're still around, busting skulls."

"Who are they?" I ask.

"One is a heavyweight, Matt Swartz, except he changed his name recently to Matt Swan so people wouldn't think he's a Kraut. I don't blame him. Anyway, he's got six wins and two losses to his credit. That's not the greatest record, but all his wins are by KO. Can't move his feet for shit, but he's got a right jab you could bust concrete with." Then he widens his eyes a bit, realizing what he said. "Sorry, ma'am. For the language, I mean."

"No offense taken," I assure him. "Who's the other one?"

"Ah, now here's a star in the making. He's a flyweight, Kelly Mahone, or Kelly 'Automatic' Mahone, as they're calling him now, on account of his punches coming like a machine gun. Skinny as Agawa's broomstick but a real student of the game, plays defense like nobody I've seen in a while."

"What's his record?" Derek asks.

"As of last week, eleven wins and precisely zero losses."

I do not admit to either of these men that I've never seen a boxing match. Baseball, at one time, threatened to enchant me, whether it was the Blues of Double A or my beloved Monarchs of the Negro American League. But those days I had my hand in the crook of a man's elbow and watched the games from bleachers that were always warm. I've not attended a game since before the war. Either way, by comparison, boxing seems far too blunt.

"…and by the sixth round or so," Penilo is saying, "he's usually got the other guy out of breath."

"Can we speak with him?" I ask.

"Sure thing. But why?"

Four days ago I suggested to Corky that I experienced extrasensory perception, like the heroine of a dime novel. Of course I was kidding. But the impulse to talk with Kelly Mahone is there before I can identify it. "I'd like to ask him about Mr. Agawa."

"Kelly won't take the news very well. He's patient in the ring but he's got a short fuse in the real world. When he hears that his benefactor is deceased…" Penilo shakes his head and smokes.

We conclude our conversation with handshakes and a promise to keep the gym family informed of any developments. Penilo tells me that Kelly Mahone is scheduled to fight tomorrow night, Saturday, giving me the details if I should choose to interview the promising young flyweight.

Once Derek and I are clear of the place, he asks, "Did we learn anything useful in there?"

"We're not finished yet. This building contains three more businesses. I'm assuming that Kaz cleaned all of them."

"So what's next?"

"There's a dead-letter office, a taxidermist, and a socialist newspaper."

"Wow. A regular rogue's gallery."

"I suppose so. We just haven't found the right rogue yet."

Derek motions toward the rattletrap elevator. "Lead on."

Chapter Eight

In Which I Follow a Dead Man's Footsteps

Derek pulls shut the elevator's accordion door. The car is narrow; our shoulders almost touch. The gears and pulleys loudly lift us toward the next floor. Into the metal wall, some past passenger has scratched I CORINTHIANS 15:51.

After a moment of silence, Derek says, "Do you happen to know the verse?"

"You're asking the wrong sinner."

He keeps his eyes straight ahead, as people do in elevators. "You're not a churchgoer?"

I have an extended answer to that—a childhood of never missing a Sunday sermon, potlucks with casseroles as a newly married woman—but instead I reply, "Let's just say I had a falling out with Management."

"Ah. Understood."

The elevator shudders to an uncertain stop. "What about you? You seem pretty upstanding and ethical."

"That's my inner Boy Scout showing through."

"Can't help that, I suppose."

"But I've also killed at least six people."

I look up at him, unsure of what to say.

"You can't see their faces when they're in the cockpit of a Messerschmitt and you're pumping bullets into it from behind, but sometimes I dream about them burning to death on the way down. So, no, I've not been to church in a while, either."

He pushes open the elevator door and leaves me two steps behind.

****

The dead-letter office is exactly that—a dead end. Through the window in the locked door, I see heaps of correspondence without recipients. Most of these letters, no doubt, remain here from the war, envelopes inscribed in poor penmanship, the notes inside written in the rain or in a bunker somewhere in muddy Belgium. An article in last week's *Life* magazine explained that there were rooms like this all over the country, repositories of unfinished lives.

We leave it. Maybe Kaz had a key and cleaned in there as part of his contract, but short of breaking down the door and pillaging the misbegotten mail for clues, we have no options here.

The next business is a socialist newspaper, *The Worker*, but apparently it recently shuttered its services. The door is unlocked, the office inside empty except for a few boxes of newsprint and a forgotten umbrella.

One floor up, we find a family business called Cordet and Sons. It seems a peculiar location for a taxidermist, but according to the telephone index, they've been stuffing dead pheasants here since 1935.

As I knock twice, Derek loosens his collar. "Going to be a scorcher today."

He's right. This stagnant hallway feels like a stovepipe.

The door opens. A bald man with bright blue eyes behind antique spectacles says, "No need to knock, friends. We're always open." He steps to the side and motions for us to enter.

I don't move. Expecting to behold an elephant head mounted to the wall or a coyote frozen in mid-lunge, my eyes flick about the scene. Instead of preserved animals, I see machines with knobs and dials, tools with bladed edges, and cables crisscrossing the floor. "I…thought this was a taxidermist's shop."

"Used to be," he says. "We've been here about six months."

"And you are?"

"My name is Antoine Cordet." He says it the fancy French way, *cor-DAY*. "I'm a crystal-grinder."

"I'm sorry. A what?"

He smiles, revealing a gap between his upper teeth. "Come on in. I'll show you."

And because it is a strange day and getting only stranger, I step inside.

****

"…and the oscillating crystal," Cordet explains, "provides a frequency reference for the radio receivers and transmitters."

I look around at the dials, boxes, coils, and cords. The devices are numerous, intricate, and obscure. "All of this equipment is for…communication?"

"Exactly. With a sufficient antenna and the right atmospheric conditions, I can send and receive messages as far away as Kathmandu—at least in theory."

"And selling these things is your business?"

"Just the crystals, mainly. A crystal's vibrations generate a signal at a precise frequency that can be changed by grinding the crystal into a particular configuration."

"So, in layman's terms—"

"A crystal needs to be shaped in order to hear anything other than static on the radio."

"And you cut them into that shape."

"Among other things, yes. I also build oscillators and teach Morse."

"Say that part again?"

"Morse code. It's one of the principal means of communicating in radio. You can't imagine the number of Morse messages sent around the globe over the last five or six years. It's an invaluable skill."

"I'm sure." I wonder if any of this would have been important to Kazuhiko. Was he as interested in radio transmissions as he was in the local boxing scene? "Can I ask you an unrelated question?"

"Definitely."

"Is a custodian employed to clean here?"

"Sure. Shows up every afternoon around four o'clock. Asian fellow."

"Do you know him?"

"Not very well. Seems friendly enough, though. He works for the building's owner." Antoine Cordet narrows his eyes behind his glasses. "Is something wrong?"

I open my mouth to explain that, yes, something is very much wrong, but I don't know how to say it in a way that doesn't make it sound too small; the murder of a kind man like Kaz should not be distilled to a sentence or two. Fortunately, Derek intervenes. In a rather military manner, he gives Cordet a summary of events, tells him that we're friends of the family and that we're here to reach out to anyone who might be affected by the tragic event. That's how he phrases it: *the tragic event*, like something out of one of the daytime radio dramas.

Cordet takes the news like we always do when learning of the death of a passing acquaintance: surprised, mildly concerned, appropriately reverent.

I forge ahead. "Did Mr. Agawa ever express interest in your work here?"

"A little, I guess, here and there. Shortwave transmission isn't a pursuit that appeals to the general population, I'm afraid. We talked about it, but never at length."

"Your customer base is fairly narrow, then?"

"We don't sell a lot of crystals to the public. There are a handful of enthusiasts in the city, hobbyists who enjoy building their own rigs. We're the only parts supplier in the area. But most of our sales are direct to Uncle Sam."

"How so?"

"The war created a considerable demand for communication equipment. Any man who can grind a crystal has a built-in market, thanks to the U.S. Army."

"It's lucrative business?"

"Well, I wouldn't go that far. *Dependable*, yes. *Steady*, yes."

"I see. You said that Mr. Agawa was employed by the building's owner."

"Yes, that's true. As part of my lease, I'm provided janitorial services."

"Who's the owner?" I don't know why it's taken me this long to ask. "What's his name?"

"Uh, Breckenridge," Cordet says. "I've never met him in person, but that's the name I write on the check each month, Wallace Breckenridge."

Again I wonder if I need to be taking notes. Jim was

never without his small, leatherbound journal, its cover frayed, its pages packed with the minutiae of the cases he worked and the list of items I sent him to fetch at the grocer's.

"May I ask how he died?" Cordet says.

Derek tells him. A bludgeon. A random attack. Probably racially motivated.

I wrap things up after that, thanking Antoine Cordet for his time and for the lessons in radio operation, as well as for the name of Wallace Breckenridge. When Derek and I are back in the elevator, he glances at his watch and says, "You'll need to be getting to work pretty soon."

"Will I?"

"Your shift starts after lunch, doesn't it?"

"I'm thinking of taking the day off."

"They'll let you do that?"

"Ms. Peele won't appreciate it."

"Who?"

"The warden of the salt mine."

"Sounds intimidating. Do you have any personal days to cash in?"

"Men receive paid time off. Women do not."

"You're willing to miss a day's pay?"

"The Agawas gave me almost a thousand dollars. My rent is twenty-nine. I'll be okay."

"That sounds like a slippery slope to quitting your job."

The elevator squeaks and stops at the ground floor—and I'm struck by the sudden need to confirm that Breckenridge also owns Corky Schneider's building. Kaz was employed to clean both. "On second thought, I'm going to work—assuming your taxi services are still available to get me there."

"Of course. Why the sudden change?"

"The index."

"What's that?"

"It's the book that's going to help me locate Wallace Breckenridge."

"So…tomorrow's agenda is Breckenridge?"

"In the morning, yes. But tomorrow night, we need to be ringside for Kelly Mahone."

Derek ratchets the elevator door open. "If I didn't know better, Mrs. Frisco, I'd say you were an old hand at all of this."

Before exiting the lift, I stop and look up at him. I could print all that I know about him on one side of a matchbox. But I'm glad he's here. "What would you be doing today if you weren't escorting me about town?"

"Oh, I don't know…" He gives a little sway on the balls of his feet. "I suppose I'd be spending my leave like any other red-blooded fellow, smoking cigars and playing five-card stud."

"I don't believe that."

The smile on his face is distant, a little pensive. "The truth of the matter is that I don't have many good friends, not anymore. And the way I see it, the safest bet right now is to keep it that way. So the answer to your question is that, without your invitation, I'd likely be changing the spark plugs in the Cord and listening to Uncle Chuck tell me about a new and bountiful fishing hole he found up near Avondale."

"How much time do you have left on leave?"

"I report back in about two weeks."

"I promise not to keep you that long."

"Then we better get moving."

I nod and head to the street, thinking of Morse code,

boxing rings, and other things I never dreamed would matter.

****

When I was twelve, a man named Joseph White Tail told my fortune. He was a member of the Sac and Fox tribe that still lives up near the Nebraska border. With a trestle table set up near a motor court, he took money in exchange for proverbs. I still remember mine, which cost my father twenty-five cents: *You will play so often in the sun that your shadow will never be lonely.*

I'm sure it was the same thing he said to every silly white girl who begged her father for a quarter. Nevertheless, it's remained with me, even though I no longer spend much time frolicking in the sun.

My line buzzes. My hand works the plugs and cables automatically. "Operator…"

Sitting here at the switchboard in a windowless room, I realize that this job isn't one I can perform for the next three decades until I retire. The women with whom I sit shoulder-to-shoulder are my friends; I know the names of their husbands and children and favorite records. We exchange baked goods on birthdays. We talk about knitting instructions in *Women's Weekly* and the rising cost of chuck roast. It's scandalous at half a dollar per pound.

"…hold the line, please."

With the assistance of the index, I now have the address for Mr. Wallace Coe Breckenridge. Tomorrow is Saturday. The newspaper says to expect temperatures in the nineties and nothing but sunny skies. Time for my shadow to stretch its legs.

Chapter Nine

In Which I Drink Tea with a Nazi Hunter

Today Derek is wearing a hat. It's a driving cap in blue wool, the same color as his eyes. He leans against the passenger's door, arms crossed, watching me approach. As for me, I have selected my outfit based on three becauses: because it is summer, because it is Saturday, and because I am doing things I've never done before. Plain flat shoes are not in vogue, and you'd never see them on the feet of Ingrid Bergman, but they are dependable.

Before I can offer so much as a good morning, Derek says, "I'm wondering if you accept gifts from men you just met."

"Well, that all hinges on the gift, I suppose."

"Coffee from Kathy Mack's diner down the street."

I smile, my first of the day. "In that case, I accept unconditionally."

Derek reaches into the convertible and produces two cups made of waxed paperboard, with foil lids.

"I hope you don't take sugar, because Kathy wouldn't let me bring the shaker with me."

"I'll be fine. Thank you."

As I remove the lid and test that first tentative sip, I move my eyes left and right, taking in the sights of my quiet neighborhood. The butcher's son is writing the daily specials on a chalkboard in front of the shop. Next door, the cobbler props his door open, an early effort against the heat. A group of boys swats a tin can along the sidewalk like a game of field hockey, their sticks perfectly sized and shaped for the activity.

"This is where I'm supposed to offer you a penny," Derek says.

"I'm sorry?"

"For your thoughts."

I shake my head. "It's nothing. I don't usually take the time to look around. But I woke up today and realized that I might miss something important if I don't pay attention to everything."

"Seems to me like the Agawas' money has gone to the right person."

I take another sip, longer this time. "I haven't helped at all."

"Maybe, maybe not." He follows my gaze. One of the boys whacks at the can like a golfer—and misses entirely, inciting laughter. "Our first stop is to see this Breckenridge fellow?"

"I've telephoned him twice this morning, but the line is occupied."

"Then we'll drop in uninvited."

"Catch him off guard?"

"That's what I'm thinking. How about you, Mrs. Frisco?"

"I'm thinking Kathy Mack makes great coffee, with or without sugar."

Derek agrees, then opens the car door for me, and a moment later we're flying.

****

I have written a script in my mind for my interview

with Wallace Breckenridge.

VIVIAN: Thank you for agreeing to meet with me, Mr. Breckenridge. May I call you Wallace?

BRECKENRIDGE: Is this going to take long?

VIVIAN: (Lights expensive cigarette, probably Turkish, exhales dramatically) Do you have somewhere else to be right now?

BRECKENRIDGE: I'm a busy man.

VIVIAN: So I've heard. I want to ask you a few questions.

BRECKENRIDGE: And if I refuse to answer?

VIVIAN: (Glances at the muscled sentry in a blue driving cap) Let's hope it doesn't come to that.

BRECKENRIDGE: So ask already.

VIVIAN: Do you own any buildings around town?

BRECKENRIDGE: Yes. That's public record.

VIVIAN: And you lease the spaces inside to various businesses?

BRECKENRIDGE: Why? Did one of my tenants do something wrong?

VIVIAN: Who cleans those buildings, Wallace?

BRECKENRIDGE: Huh?

VIVIAN: You do have the properties cleaned occasionally, don't you?

BRECKENRIDGE: (perturbed) Of course. I use a guy.

VIVIAN: A guy?

BRECKENRIDGE: A Jap with a name I can't pronounce. Is there anything else?

VIVIAN: One more question.

BRECKENRIDGE: Lay it on me.

VIVIAN: (crushes out cigarette) Where were you on the morning of July second?

BRECKENRIDGE: (nervously) I was just, uh…I happened to be—

"Mrs. Frisco?"

I blink to find Derek looking at me from the driver's seat. "I'm sorry?"

"I said we're here."

So we are. The Cord idles in front of a multilevel brick home with ornamented eaves, circa 1920. It might have been Jay Gatsby's getaway, had the fictional gadabout ever been inclined to vacation in humble Kansas City.

I don't wait for Derek, ever the gentleman, to open my door for me.

****

Until today, I have never been in the same room as a swastika.

A captured Nazi flag hangs behind glass, one corner burned away. The thing is huge. An entire wall opposite the fireplace is hidden by a frame that must be at least fifteen feet long and half as high. It's as impressive as it is startling.

Wallace Breckenridge has spent the last seven minutes telling us of his part in the Battle of Aachen in October two years back. He was a member of the 743rd Tank Battalion.

"We ripped the flag from the Hotel Quellenhof," he says, hands in his trouser pockets as we stare up at the monstrosity. "I paid a rug merchant in France to see that it was shipped back to the States."

After all of that, I'm not sure what to say. "It's…intimidating."

Beside me, Derek turns away from the improbably large banner. His face looks chipped from stone. He finds some less ghastly mementoes atop a bookshelf and fixes his attention there.

"...though I feel as if it's a reminder of all that was almost lost that day."

"It's certainly a conversation piece," I admit, before following Derek's lead and averting my eyes.

Breckenridge serves us iced tea and gets us settled into wicker chairs on his patio. He's a middle-aged man with a middle-aged paunch, his haircut military, his Windsor knot slightly askew. The Saturday morning sun shines through our dark drinks and turns them gold.

For the next few minutes, we move from introductions and pillaged flags to why we've come. Between the two of us, Derek and I manage to take the sharp truth—*a man is dead and we're here for answers*—and blunt it with euphemism and circumspection.

"Did you know him?" I eventually ask. "Kazuhiko Agawa?"

"Never met the man. Sorry to hear about his loss, just the same. Now that you mention it, I recall reading something in the paper a few days ago. Didn't think much of it."

"I was led to believe that he cleaned your buildings."

Breckenridge nods as he takes a drink, then wipes his mouth on his sleeve. "That may very well be true. I have no idea who does the actual cleaning of the three properties."

"How is that possible?"

"I employ a domestic service."

"A cleaning company?"

"That's right. Heavenly Households, it's called. Been using them for years."

And then, as clearly as one of those clarinet notes through my window at night, a notion occurs to me. I silently add a few lines to my script.

VIVIAN: (stares across steepled fingers, professionally manicured) A man was murdered four days ago in a building you own, and you didn't hear about it until you read it in the paper?

BRECKENRIDGE: Well, um…what I meant to imply was that, uh—

I go ahead and say it—"I'm sorry, Mr. Breckenridge, but you were unaware of the murder until you saw the newspaper story the next morning?"

"That's right."

"The police didn't call to inform you that someone died on your property?"

He tilts toward me in his seat, the ice tinkling in his mostly empty glass. "Actually, I wasn't aware of it until this very moment. The story in the paper didn't mention the location."

"It wasn't much of a story, just a single paragraph." *He's a Jap and nobody cares.* "But I was there. An attorney named Corky Schneider found the body."

"Schneider? That would be the Horizon building. My father built it in 1907. It's mostly vacant, still waiting for tenants to start showing up again. It was practically abandoned during the war. You're sure?"

"I saw the police in the lobby that morning. Why wouldn't they call you?"

"Why would they?"

"You own the place where a man was murdered."

Breckenridge sets his glass down on a side table and sits up straight. "I'm sorry, ma'am, but why exactly are you here?"

"We're friends of the Agawa family."

"If you're looking for answers, I'm afraid I can't help you. I had no idea that anyone died in the Horizon building. Now if you don't mind—"

Derek nods on my behalf and offers a friendly smile that seems out of place, given the look that Breckenridge is leveling at me. "Our apologies. It's an emotional time for all of us. We certainly didn't mean to imply anything."

I know what's coming next. The two men in the room exchange glances—

DEREK: Sorry about that, old chap. Broads, you know.

BRECKENRIDGE: Don't mention it, dear fellow. We make allowances for the emotions of the fairer sex.

—and I am promptly forgotten, which is probably for the best, considering the cinders in my heart.

We are not allowed to leave quickly. Half an hour passes. Now that Derek is steering the ship, he permits Wallace Breckenridge to indulge himself, showing off his collection of ceremonial sabers and lamenting the slow return of post-war industry to the heartland.

"The stock market's in a tailspin," Breckenridge says.

"I'm hearing it may be months before it rebounds," Derek adds.

"Indeed. Ever since the stock regulators raised the market margin requirements in January, we've seen nothing but wholesale sell-offs."

They go on like this, back and forth like friendly badminton players at the athletics club, while I try to convince myself that my time here isn't wasted.

Before we leave, I ask only one more question: "Mr.

Breckenridge, did you say you own *three* buildings?"

"That's right. The Horizon, the Benton Street building, and a warehouse on the river that's unfortunately been as empty as a ghost town for the last two years. Business is bound to pick up again, I'm sure."

Derek holds open my car door but doesn't look at me as he says, "Thanks for having us, sir. And for showing off those swords. It's been a pleasure."

It ends shortly after that. The two of them trade more *lingua male* and chuckle about something of no interest to me. Breckenridge probably comments on the Cord, and Derek grins humbly but not humbly enough to conceal his agreement that yes, it's a right-on proper automobile.

When we're a mile down the road, the wind rushing over us like a sea current, he loosens his collar and says, "Sorry about that."

"There's no need to—"

"There is, actually. Men like Breckenridge prefer women to be seen but not…you know. I don't want to be one of them."

"Thoughtful of you to say. But you probably saved me from doing something rash."

"Like what?"

"Like asking more questions that I shouldn't ask."

"Seems like a dead end to me. Breckenridge wasn't even aware that someone had passed away on his property."

"So he says."

Derek turns his head toward me, his driving cap just above his eyes. "You think he's lying?"

"Somebody is."

"Who? Antoine Cordet the crystal-grinder? Vic

Penilo the boxing promoter?"

I point toward the highway in front of us. "Best to keep your vision on the road."

The miles roll beneath us. Derek taps his fingers on the wheel. "You know, Mrs. Frisco, the simplest answer is usually the correct one."

"So they say."

"A lot of people in this country hate the Japanese— with good reason. Take a fellow with a bad temper, one with a history of violence, and then tell him that his brother who serves in the navy has been blown up by a suicidal Zero pilot in a surprise attack...that type of man might see it as a kind of revenge to strike out at a janitor with the wrong shape of eyes."

I stare from the window. "I know. But...if it was just some random act, I'll never find who did it."

"Not everything is a conspiracy."

"Mrs. Agawa paid me."

"This isn't about the money."

"No, Mr. O'Brien, it's not." Finally I turn to look at him. "It's about her. It's about what she lost. And I'm sure that Freud would say it's somehow about me, too. Now, I know you're probably right about everything, but at least take me to the boxing matches tonight so I can meet Kelly Mahone."

"And then what?"

"And then I'm done. If Mr. Mahone can't give us anything, then I'll mail the money back to the Agawa family so we can all get on with our lives. Is that good enough for you?"

He considers it, flexing his fingers on the Cord's leather-wrapped steering wheel. After a while he says, "How about a stop at Kathy Mack's on the way back?

You can treat for lunch with your ill-gotten gains."

It sounds like the best offer I'm bound to get. "Deal."

****

Two hours later, I'm back at the switchboard, pretending at an ordinary life.

Lunch with Derek went like this:

Once upon a time, two mostly strangers ate pastrami on rye at the corner diner and enumerated on a napkin the extent of their knowledge—(1) a dead custodian, (2) the building where he died, (3) the cleaning service for which he worked, (4) the boxing gym he patronized, (5) the Morse code expert with whom he chatted, and (6) the wealthy war veteran who owned the location of his death.

Derek observed that it didn't add up to anything at all.

Unable to disagree with him, I finished my sandwich and a side of potato salad, paying the waitress with money I hadn't earned.

Now I have only one trail left to follow before I give in to good sense, the Saturday-evening boxing card and an undefeated flyweight.

As soon as my shift is over, I gather my hat, gloves, and handbag, offering little more than a nod when the girl from the incoming shift wishes me goodnight. This is fight night—my first. And I don't intend to miss it.

Chapter Ten

In Which I Help the Bucket-Man

At the corner of 13th and Central stands Municipal
Auditorium, constructed ten years ago to replace the
aging Convention Hall where I had my first summer job
as a cigarette girl during an annual meeting of traveling
salesmen. That was a lifetime ago, a year after Ace
Norris's family moved away. I remember walking
around with a tray at my waist, proffering a selection of
tobacco products to men who sold laxatives from their
cars.

Underneath the nighttime sky, the marquee reads
HEAVYWEIGHTS COLLIDE!

Derek and I stand in one of two lines at the ticket
booth. The top-billed fight is Gary "Goliath" Bradshaw
against the 250-pound V.V. Jones from Winona,
Mississippi. The bookies have Bradshaw at 3:2 odds,
giving him the slight edge over a bigger opponent,
probably because he's Caucasian, so it is likely to go
either way. The betting is lively.

"Looks like our man is third on the card," Derek
observes. He's changed into sporting attire while I was
at work. He wears a dark blue coat over a striped shirt,
like the captain of a catamaran. He has had time for an
evening shave. He smells of sandalwood cologne.

As for me, I came here straight from the telephone

exchange, so I'm wearing the same outfit as this morning at the Breckenridge house, but I've had the good sense to unpin my hair. "So the lighter-weight classes fight first?"

"That's right. There are two amateur bouts, then Kelly Mahone."

At the box, I pay eighty cents for a pair of tickets in the seventh row.

The coliseum has the usual two entrances. We head toward the one for whites only, but all the laughter, all the joviality, all the excited talk of an upset for the fighter from Winona, is coming from the other line, where folks seem to be having a much better time.

****

We do not advance directly to our seats. Earlier, in the car, I suggested to Derek that we seek out Mr. Mahone before the bout. Having never attended a boxing match, I'm not sure what condition the combatants will be in when it's over. For all I know, Kelly "Automatic" Mahone will be borne from the ring on a stretcher and be of no use to me at all.

So Derek asks some questions of the attendants and gets a few nods toward an area at the periphery, accessed by gray metal doors. I assume these are the locker rooms, where men plan the destruction of each other, where the tinder of dreams tries to catch fire before it's snuffed.

We walk behind the farthest row of folding chairs. Under floodlights at the center of the auditorium, the ring waits, a twenty-foot square surrounded by four sets of sagging ropes. Two boys wipe the canvas down. The seats begin to fill.

The young man at the door—likely a college student doing night work—shakes his head as we approach.

"Sorry, folks. Nobody back here but trainers and such. House rules."

"I understand," says Derek, as if he's not at all surprised to find our way blocked. "But it's important we have a few moments with someone before the bouts. We'll just be a minute."

"Wish I could, sir. But the insurance companies make the rules."

"Since when did insurance companies get involved in the small-town fight scene?"

"Beats me. Just repeating what I was told. If you want to plead your case, you can head upstairs to the office and—"

I interrupt him. "How much will it cost us to get back there?"

"Ma'am?"

I extend a ten-dollar bill. "Why don't you go have a smoke?"

He looks at the money, then at me. Then he snaps the cash away and pulls the cigarettes from his sleeve. "You folks enjoy the fights." He leaves us alone with the doors.

We watch him go.

"You're getting good at this," Derek says.

"Maybe I am."

Derek ushers me deeper inside.

****

A few minutes later, I am making the acquaintance of Kelly Mahone. We stand in a windowless room with concrete walls and very little ventilation. Mahone sits on a metal bench, getting his arms rubbed down by his trainer. His blond hair is cut short. His blue eyes are deep and crackle with life. His face is too young for scars but he has one anyway, a half-moon on his chin. He is beautifully American.

"Mr. Mahone?"

He wears a white robe a size too large. "The one and only. Who's asking?"

By now I've mastered our introduction, the who-we-are and the why-we're-here, but this time when I mention being friends of the Kazuhiko Agawa family, I receive an instant look of recognition and grief.

"So you know what happened?" I ask.

"I know he's dead, if that's what you mean. Agawa was my friend, and some shitbag murdered him."

Mahone doesn't apologize for the language, and I don't expect him to. Since leaving the funeral, I haven't met anyone who shares the warmth of my anger, until now.

"They catch who did it?" he asks.

"We're trying to help with that."

"Oh, yeah? How's that?"

"Do you have any idea who might be responsible?"

"I wish. If I had the asshole that murdered him in front of me right now, I'd get a little payback, or maybe a lot."

"I understand. Mr. Mahone, my friend and I—"

"Call me Kelly. Save the *misters* for the old men."

"All right, Kelly. We just need perhaps two minutes of your time."

"Clock's ticking. I can't afford any distractions. This here's my last fight before going to New York. They figure I'm two, maybe three wins away from getting a shot at the title."

"That's impressive. Who's the current champion?"

"A Scotsman named Jackie Paterson. Guy's a

southpaw, if you can believe it."

"Can you beat him?"

Kelly grins, his smile immaculate. "If it's God's will."

"Is God a boxing fan?"

"If you're talking about the Old Testament, then yeah, I think He'd be ringside."

"How long did you know Mr. Agawa?"

"Over a year. Solid guy. Backed me up more than once. Had a lot of good advice. Never expected to hear wisdom from a mop-jockey, you know?"

"When was the last time you saw him?"

"The day before he died, he was in the gym emptying trashcans."

"How did you hear about his death?"

"The papers. Same as everybody else, I guess."

"Vic Penilo told me that Mr. Agawa supported your career."

"Hell, yeah. Guy stood in my corner for the last few fights, helped out a lot. I can't exactly afford much of a support staff—at least not yet."

"Did you ever meet his family or know any of his other friends?"

What Kelly says next changes everything.

"Nah, nothing like that. I never had supper at his house or drank a beer with him. But when Agawa needed a favor, I didn't hesitate."

I shift my weight slightly from one foot to another. "May I ask what kind of favor?"

"The enforcer kind."

"Pardon?"

Kelly flexes his thickly taped fingers. "Look, I gotta get ready for the fight, so here's the short version." His trainer ices his shoulders. "One day Agawa comes to the gym, and instead of going for his broom he comes straight to me. Says he wants to talk. We use Vic's office for privacy. Agawa says he needs to meet some people that night, and the meeting's at this abandoned warehouse on the river and it might not be safe. He asks me to come along in case things get out of hand. So I go. Got no idea what to expect. We end up in this big building and something like four or five Jap families are living in there, in secret, you know, on account of their houses getting burned down."

I nod my understanding. I've heard the stories. It used to just be the Ku Klux Klan that did that sort of thing. Not anymore.

Meanwhile, Kelly's trainer—a stoop-shouldered man with a ring of red hair—begins tugging big horsehair-filled gloves onto his fighter's hands.

"What happened next?" I ask.

"These two other guys show up," Kelly says, "and as soon as I see them, I understand why Agawa wanted reinforcements. I don't know where they were from—Chicago, most likely—but they were the kind of heavies you see in a James Cagney picture, if you get what I'm saying."

"What did they want?"

"Money. They wanted the families to pay up."

"What for?"

"Protection racket. Either money exchanged hands or else."

I process that for a few seconds. "So…I'm guessing that they refused to pay. Did anyone get hurt?"

He grins. "None of the good guys."

"I see. Did the police get involved?"

"Are you kidding? The cops treat the Japs worse than they treat the Negroes." Suddenly he stands up. I realize he's no taller than I am. "Sorry, but duty calls and all that."

His trainer says, "Boy needs to focus."

I ignore him. "When was the meeting?"

"About a week ago."

"In a warehouse on the Missouri?"

"Yeah."

In my mind, Wallace Breckenridge says, *The Horizon, the Benton Street building, and a warehouse on the river that's unfortunately been as empty as a ghost town for the last two years.*

Derek touches my arm. "Let's go find our seats."

"Thank you, Kelly."

"Don't mention it."

I allow Derek to lead me away as I build a scaffold of evidence in my mind. Kaz worked at Heavenly Households, which was under contract to clean Breckenridge's properties. That's how he learned of the warehouse and knew it was empty. He smuggled his friends and their families inside, giving them a place to stay while they made arrangements to relocate somewhere more accepting of their—

"Hey, wait a minute," Kelly calls.

We turn back.

Kelly nods at Derek. "Think you could be my bucket-man?"

"Come again?" Derek says.

"Agawa was supposed to be my bucket-man tonight. So I need another set of hands in my corner." He looks at his trainer. "That all right with you, Hal?"

Hal waves his hands. "Fine. He'll do. Let's just get

out there before we get DQ'ed for not showing up."

"What's a bucket-man?" I ask.

Derek guides me out of the way as Kelly Mahone and his trainer leave the room, the young flyweight shaking his shoulders and bouncing on the balls of his feet.

"From what I understand," Derek says, "a bucket-man stands in a fighter's corner and, well—"

"Holds a bucket?"

"I believe so."

"What for?"

"Spitting blood, primarily."

"That's disgusting."

Derek smiles. "I'm honored to do my part. Besides, I can't let you have all the fun."

"This isn't fun."

"Not even a little?" He doesn't expect a reply. "Shall we?"

I rest my hand lightly in his elbow, like a woman with her fingertips on the prow of a ship.

****

In the future, if someone asks me to describe this night, I will use the word *erotic*. Not in a sexual sense. But there is an intimacy to be found in the ring, two exhausted strangers half-clutching each other and leaning into the ropes for a few moments of ragged breathing. Their paths may never cross again after tonight, but right now, they are all that matters to each other. It starts with the two amateurs, desperate young men wearing almost no clothing, flailing as if to fight their way from obscurity. Their hunger is sensual and boyish at once.

Those first two fights stun me into silence. Because

Derek is now part of Kelly's crew, they have seated us in the very front, directly behind his corner. I'm wide-eyed at the spectacle and sweating lightly into my blouse.

Derek turns to me. "What do you think?"

I look around at the crowd, a couple of hundred strong. I may be the only woman here. Boxing is a man's game. I imagine in the larger cities, the big players bring their molls along, women awash in pearls and perfunctory smiles. But here in the Midwest, ladies have more sensible places to be. It's pinochle night at Betty's house, for example.

"It's beautiful and wild," I reply.

Kelly Mahone's bout begins after his name is announced by an energized radio man in front of a large microphone. Someone strikes a steel bell. And then the flurry.

Kelly and his opponent arabesque into one another, dancing and stabbing. Kelly's punches happen nearly too quickly for me to see. Even as he strikes, his feet shift him out of the way of any riposte, so that he seems to move two directions at the same time, both attacker and evader. Two minutes into the first round, it's clear even to me that his barrage will not be equaled here, at least not by this unfortunate fellow tonight.

The man in the seat behind me frames it ineloquently yet accurately: "*Kid's beating the salt and shit out of him*." The bell ends the round.

Derek is ready. He leaps to Kelly's corner, bucket in hand.

Compelled by the spirit of it all, I follow, and my unlikely evening continues.

Chapter Eleven

In Which I Break the Fourth Wall

My breakfast the next morning consists of a single cup of coffee, next to which is a stenographer's pad that has become my version of Jim's casebook. I do not think of him as I list my notes chronologically down the page. I do not recall his scent as I record names and addresses and draw connecting lines between them. I do not remember the way he slept with his head in the crook of his elbow when I close the notebook and lean back in my chair.

A moment passes. Then I turn my head slightly and look right at you.

Yes, you. You're the one seeing this all through my brown eyes, the one walking in my inexpensive but serviceable shoes, and so it's only fair of me to warn you directly. Life is full of airless places. No one can breathe for you. You suffocate a little, on certain mornings. And then you stand up and take in those breaths, one at a time, each one putting you fractionally farther away from the sorrow.

I do the same, smoothing my skirt. I break eye contact and let you off the hook—at least for now.

Taking up my notebook, my money, and my favorite hat, I head downstairs to the street, hopefully ready for whatever happens next.

****

"You're not worried about an atomic war?" Derek asks.

My arm rests on the Cord's door frame as we drive, the convertible top stowed away, the sun everywhere around us. "The radio news tells me that no one knows how to make a bomb but us. Or does the Air Corps know something the rest of us don't?"

"The brass are saying it's only a matter of time."

I keep my eyes on the passing scenery, the shops of Kansas City scrolling by like the images seen in a nickelodeon theater. "Is this the usual sunny subject matter for airmen on leave?"

"Boys will be boys, I suppose."

I turn my head toward him, my hat in my lap so it doesn't blow away. Today he's wearing a khaki shirt with epaulets, the sleeves rolled to his elbows. I notice a scar on his right arm. "Perhaps we should change the subject to something more appropriate."

"Would love to. What did you have in mind?"

"Oh, I don't know. What do men think that women talk about?"

He shoots me a glance, then looks back at the street. "A wise man here would keep his mouth shut."

"Dinner parties?" I suggest. "Or how to bake a ham? Or nylons?"

"Nylons?"

"Stockings, dear man. How's that for a conversation topic? Do you prefer to hold them up with garters made of rayon or cotton?"

"Mrs. Frisco, I believe that you're teasing me."

"Cotton, is it? I suspected as much." I give an exaggerated sigh and return my attention to the scenery.

When I chance a peek at him, he's grinning.

Ten minutes later we arrive at the warehouse where Kaz was hiding his exiled Japanese friends.

****

There are two kinds of places in this town. One of them is new, post-war, proud of itself and ready to carry us all toward the 1950s. These buildings are typically full of windows and vented throughout for some kind of centralized heating or cooling system—novel stuff. The paint is predictably patriotic. The other type is a carryover, neglected for at least five years, the way our relationships have been neglected, like a relative from your mother's side to whom you've not spoken since 1939. Kaz's secret refuge, owned by Wallace Breckenridge, is an expansive metal storehouse that leans against the riverbank as if considering sliding all the way in and getting it over with. We are beyond the city limits, in the farmland fringes that have been abandoned or overlooked in recent years. No one ventures out to these roads except teenagers hoping to race their daddy's cars or boys yearning to get their hands up their girlfriend's sweaters.

We park near the water's edge. My father fished in this river. My mother would take the paddlefish or channel cat he caught and bread them with flour and thyme, then fry them in a black skillet that was supposedly as old as the Civil War. The flavor returns to my mouth with surprising clarity.

"Coming?"

I put on my hat and join him. In the river behind me, dazzling fish go uncaught.

We approach from the east. The ground here is packed earth. In a past life, this was a parking lot, with trucks moving back and forth to load or unload whatever was once stocked here, but now the only vehicles are two that will never move again. They seem mostly made of weeds.

"Do you see a door?" Derek asks.

There is no entry point in sight, but I have already noticed something I don't like. The overgrown sedges that lead to the river have been trampled down in visible trails, and this passage seems to have happened fairly recently. Someone has been regularly moving back and forth.

We make our way along one of the building's walls, which are fashioned of concrete blocks and corrugated steel. The few windows are nothing but wooden sheets set into teeth of broken glass. The path of trampled weeds angles toward the riverbank. No vessel is moored there—at least not anymore. Whatever business is being conducted here is the type that avoids the dockmaster's log book.

Perhaps sensing my unease, Derek drops his voice to a whisper: "What's the matter?"

I shake my head and indicate that we should continue our search for the warehouse door. I don't confide in him that this is the first time since accepting Mrs. Agawa's money that I have felt not entirely certain of my safety.

We turn the corner, now on the building's north face, the side opposite the river. Cigarette butts litter the ground. They do not look very old. Are these the kind of observations that add up to something? Has Derek noticed anything?

There will be time for those questions later. We have found our door.

Two of them, actually, one broad and barn-style and the other a standard steel rectangle the color of rust. We walk those last few feet in total silence. Then we stand and listen. Any possible sounds from the other side are obscured by the flute of wind through old pipes and the river shrugging against the shore.

Before giving Derek a nod to open the door, I look at you once more. Never forget the gravity days, the way it feels to want to sink, the numbing comfort of the hole into which you've slowly descended. When you finally start to crawl out, elbows dirty, you'll want to remember, so as never to allow yourself to go back.

This will be the last time we speak, you and I. From this point forward, you're on your own.

Chapter Twelve

In Which I Find a Red-and-Blue Clue

A few days ago, a woman in France wore a two-piece swimsuit called a *bikini*. I saw it in the paper. She looked like she was walking on the beach in her underwear, and she was exceptionally pleased with herself. The news editor issued an apology the next morning for perpetuating the scandal. He was probably fired. Unsurprisingly, the bikini was designed by a man.

I think about this as Derek pushes open the warehouse door because he mentioned an atomic war during our drive here. Many are saying that the splitting of the atom signals the end of the world, a discovery so terrible that the human race is now stampeding toward the book of Revelation. That French fashion designer named his risqué swimwear after Bikini Atoll, a cluster of islands where our government is testing its bomb.

The only human beings who have ever been targeted by these weapons are the Japanese, and now two dozen of them are staring at me in various states of alarm.

They live here. That much is obvious by the clothing that hangs on lines strung between steel beams and the beds built on wooden shelves. The vast space is illuminated by a perimeter of skylights in the ceiling, aided by the glow of lanterns in a corner dedicated as a kitchen. The makeshift stove is a fifty-gallon barrel with a door cut into it and a galvanized pipe for a chimney to vent the fumes.

I turn my head cautiously. They look back at me, several families, kids and grandparents, cousins and aunts, tidy people living out of suitcases arrayed on onion crates against the wall.

They seem to have solidified. Like deer, they hope that complete stillness will prompt us to move on and let them be. They have decorated each living space with the wildflowers that grow in abundance near the river, pinks and azure blues with soda bottles for vases.

If I'm waiting for Derek to speak up, I'll apparently find no assistance there. So, not eloquently at all, I clear my throat and say, "Good morning."

What follows isn't really silence. Birds converse outside; an elderly man coughs into his elbow; my heart beats. But it's annoying just the same, so I take one step forward and appoint a spokesman by locking eyes with a random man in pince-nez glasses. "I'm Mrs. Frisco. This is my colleague, Mr. O'Brien. Kazuhiko Agawa was a friend of mine. I'm here on behalf of his family."

There, that's better. They thaw out, exchanging glances and a nod or two. One of the children—he can't be more than six—lifts a hand and waves, and then is folded in behind the leg of his mother.

"Hello," the man in the glasses finally says, and then nothing else. Clearly I picked the wrong person.

I look at Derek, who shrugs, and I'm just about to plant my hands on my hips and increase my volume when a voice from the corner says, "I told them we should've bolted the door."

I turn to see a Japanese man in his twenties, perched in a nook between crates halfway up the wall, like a pirate lookout in the crow's nest. He's in his stocking feet—like all the rest of them. He holds a book, the skylight directly above him. After marking his place in the pages, he descends easily, then approaches after saying a few words in Japanese to the rest of the group.

He looks at Derek. "You knew Mr. Agawa?"

"Never met the man." Derek tips his head at me.

"Kaz was my friend," I confirm, which is more or less true. *Acquaintance* would be more accurate. "And you are?"

"Jesse Imada, Princeton class of 1938, co-captain of the debate team, and shogun in exile." He smiles a bit at this part, then bows in the traditional way.

"A pleasure to meet you."

He speaks with no accent. "That's my mom and pops there, Akari and Haruto. We were sent to an internment center in New Mexico during the war, just in case we had any spying and sabotage in mind. I was born in San Francisco, not that it mattered."

"Why are you here? In this place?"

"We were evicted. They took our house."

"Who did?"

"The fair city of Denver, where we relocated after leaving the camp. The kind white councilmen found it in our best interest to remove us from the vicinity of our neighbors, in case we were offending someone by the way we trimmed our grass."

"That was legal?"

"You've obviously not met the Denver district attorney."

"And the rest of these people?"

"Different verses of the same song. Their shops were ransacked. Their kids were beaten up. Their jobs were taken away." He crosses his arms in a semi-challenging way. "You're telling me you haven't heard about any of this?"

"It doesn't make the news, no."

"Newspapers aren't owned by slant-eyes, I guess."

"I beg your pardon, sir. Don't implicate me in any of that."

He relaxes, then nods. "Fair enough. Let's start over. Name's Jesse." He holds out his hand.

"Vivian." We shake.

"I heard they killed Kazuhiko."

"Who's they?"

He shrugs. "You tell me. Come on. I'll introduce you to the dispossessed."

I meet fifteen of them in all. They are demure, polite, and capable of smiles they probably don't feel. They represent four different families who'd never met before the war, business-owners and housewives, every one of them an English-speaking American citizen, all of them tired of showing their papers to prove it. Derek and I have taken off our shoes, respecting what is apparently a cultural custom.

"I was working in publishing when I got the notice," Jesse says, hands in the pockets of his well-fitting chinos. "I was told that my department was downsizing. As a junior editor, I was the logical choice on the chopping block."

"I'm sorry to hear that."

"They hired someone to take my place two days later, very blond, very round eyes."

"How did you end up in Kansas City?"

"Word gets around."

"Word of what, exactly?"

"Are you familiar with the Underground Railroad?"

"Not really. Something about the Civil War and slaves, I think."

"Same principle. There's a group of Japanese sympathizers who help people find jobs, move on with life."

"Why here?"

"It's centrally located. We have refugees coming from both coasts—refugees in our own country. At any rate, if you came to tell us about Kazuhiko, we already know. Like I said, word gets around."

"How was he involved in this?"

"What does it matter?"

"It matters because he left family members behind who want answers."

"And they sent you?"

"Actually, yes."

"Interesting. You're not a police officer."

"How would you know I'm not?"

"Are they hiring women now?"

"About as frequently as they hire Japanese."

He smiles. It is the kind of smile that has no pretense, no backstory. "A freelancer, huh?"

"Something like that."

"And your escort?"

I glance back. Derek is talking to a pair of men across the room, pantomiming the swing of a golf club, so he seems to have found common ground. "My bodyguard."

"You have a bodyguard? That's cool."

"It's what?"

The smile is back again. "Sorry. Saxophonist slang. The perils of hanging around with musicians. Here, have a seat."

The dinette table is neatly kept, holding a salt and pepper set with shakers in the form of little chefs, one wearing an S on its hat and the other a P. Jesse pours tea.

"How do you heat the water?" I ask. "I wouldn't think there was utility service out here."

"Very perceptive. We have wood and coal. It's funny how swiftly we've reverted to our primitive roots. Sugar?"

I nod, trying to prioritize my questions. Something tells me that Jesse Imada will divulge only what he thinks is necessary in order to keep his people safe. "How was Kaz involved in what's happening here?"

"He was local. We needed him. He knew people."

"What people?"

"The ones with the jobs, the ones who don't have a problem employing Asians."

"What kind of jobs?"

"Oh, fishing boats. Or salesmen on the telephone. The kind of choice employment in which no one can see your face. You get to be anonymously American, with no one the wiser. Dr. Jiro Kojima over there was a professor of applied mathematics and now he'll end up selling subscriptions to the *Saturday Evening Post* over the telephone."

"So Kaz arranged meetings between the...refugees and potential employers?"

"Something like that. How's your tea?"

"Delicious. What do you mean?"

"Kazuhiko was a janitor who never graduated from high school. If he'd had any strong connections in industry, he probably would have used them for his own advantage."

I spend a few seconds doing two things simultaneously: One, I study Jesse's face. His black hair is a little long, evidence that he's not had the luxury of a barber visit for a while. His cheeks are smooth. His complexion is better than mine. Two, I try to frame my next question so it doesn't sound like I'm accusing him of withholding information. "Why is it that you introduced me to your friends and offered me tea instead of throwing me out for trespassing? Aren't you afraid I'll expose you to the building's owner and get you evicted?"

"What can I say? Hospitality is our inheritance. Though I've never been to Japan, I appreciate our ancestral insistence on civility. We call it *omotenashi*. We're socially obligated to be nice to visitors, even those who arrive without invitation and start poking around."

Across the room, Derek is talking to the man whom Jesse identified as the math teacher.

"Can I pay you for your truthfulness?" I ask.

Jesse seems amused by this. "I can probably be bribed. Our senior year, I wrote Kirby Garret's term paper in exchange for a Fats Waller record."

I lean forward, teacup in both hands. "Mrs. Agawa sent me here to find out what happened to her husband. If you know anything about him that will help me give her an answer, then I'll pay you whatever you want."

He interlaces his fingers in front of his face, which ages him. There's something about that gesture that lends one temporary gravitas; I'll have to remember that. "I don't need your money. It's like this. Kazuhiko Agawa believed in *ikigai*, which doesn't really translate well into English but basically it's a respect for one's own reason to be alive. You have this thing that you live for, this reflection of your true self here in the physical world. Maybe it's your art or your career or the way you nurture your grandchildren. That's *ikigai*."

"So Kaz's purpose was...helping people?"

"I'd agree with that."

"How did he help them *specifically*?"

"First, he found this place for us. Originally we'd been living in some apartments within city limits, places that had been empty since the war, but Dr. Kojima thought it was too conspicuous. Kazuhiko suggested we relocate out here. I'm not sure how he knew about this old building."

I don't bother to relate details of Wallace Breckenridge's connection to the domestic service that employed Kaz. I sense that I'm finally closing my fist around an answer that has been eluding my grasp for days. "And beyond that? What else did he do?"

"Well, second, he stepped up when some men tried to take advantage of us."

"How so?"

"There were these guys a few days back, showed up wanting money in exchange for...I don't know, for not exposing us, for not running us off, for not beating the hell out of us—that kind of thing."

With that bit of information in place, I assemble the rest of the pieces. "And the next time those men paid you a visit, Kaz was here, and this time he didn't come alone. He brought reinforcements."

"How do you know that?"

"Is it true?"

Jesse nods. "His friend didn't seem very impressive at first. He wasn't any bigger than I am. And clearly I'm not the only one who underestimated him."

"What happened?"

"Honestly, it occurred so fast that I'm not sure. Somebody said the wrong thing, I guess, and before I realized what was going on, one of the men was on his knees, and blood was pouring out of his nose."

"Was there a fight?"

"I wouldn't call it a fight. They left after that."

"Who were these men?"

"No idea."

"They wanted money?"

"Yes."

"You didn't get any names?"

"No."

"You've never seen them before?"

"Hey, it's not like they were going to announce their entire agenda to us before shaking us down."

"I understand, but I need a way to find out who they are."

"I suppose one of them was wearing the same coat both times he showed up."

"He wore a coat in July?"

"Oh, not like that. It was a uniform jacket, like the kind worn by guys who work at a filling station."

"Was there a company name or logo on it?"

"Not that I remember. But it was blue with red stripes."

"That's it?"

"I'm not sure what you expect me to say. One of them walked out of here with a broken nose. I didn't exactly think to ask them for photo identification."

Derek gives me a gesture from across the room, a bit of telepathy that says, *Have we learned anything helpful yet?*

I reply with a one-shoulder shrug, swallow the last

of my tea, and offer Jesse Imada a polite going-away smile. "Before I leave, I don't suppose there's any chance that someone else here could provide me with any additional details about the two extortionists?"

"Unlikely. How will you locate a man based simply on the color of his coat?"

"The universe owes me. It's time I collected the debt."

"I hope you do. And your *ikigai*?"

"My reason for being?" I'm taken aback by the question. "No one's ever asked me that before."

"Maybe it's time you figure it out."

"Maybe so. Thank you for your information, Mr. Imada."

"Until next time, Mrs. Frisco." I expect him to bow, but instead he favors me one last time with that boy-like smile, a blessing for my road ahead.

I never see him again.

Chapter Thirteen

In Which I Call in Sick

This lusty Cord Phaeton, I decide as the air rushes by, would look better in red. I do not mention this to the car's owner as we hurtle into the city.

"What happens next?" Derek asks, loudly enough to be heard over the wind.

"I report to work after lunch."

"Sorry to hear that."

"I'm actually looking forward to my shift today."

"Ms. Peele is growing on you?"

"Hardly. That woman eats her oatmeal without sugar or cinnamon."

"Plain oatmeal says a lot about a person, I guess."

"There's a resource I have at a work, a collection of every telephone code in the area. I'm going to contact filling stations and oil companies and ask them an absurd question."

"And what question is that?"

"The color of their employees' uniforms."

"Sounds like a tedious task."

"What will you do? While I'm at work, I mean."

"Uncle Chuck wants me to help him sort hubcaps and set up a display of road maps in the shop lobby."

"Now *that* sounds like a tedious task. Shall we talk afterwards about what to do next?" Before he responds,

I add, "Should I feel guilty about taking up so much of your time?"

"The answers to those are yes and no." He doesn't look away from the road, but he smiles, and I admit to myself that his profile might be considered, in certain circles, handsome.

And that is my only admission for now.

****

My exchange with Ms. Peele that afternoon is best summarized as follows:

And why, exactly, do you need the index?

I don't want to take it home, Ms. Peele. But during my cigarette break—

You've taken up smoking?

Not regularly, no. But I'd like to use that time to conduct research.

For your law classes, I presume?

That's correct. My assignment is to reach out to area business with a survey.

A survey over the telephone?

Yes, ma'am.

And if one of our other operators requires the records at that time?

I'll be right here. I'll use it only when it's not needed by someone else.

At this point she pauses, assuring herself that nothing untoward could arise from this innocent request, and meanwhile I scold myself for the lies I'm so easily distributing.

Very well. Perhaps one day when you're a powerful attorney you can return the favor.

And then Ms. Peele allows herself a grin, which warms me, and I thank her with a sincerity I hadn't felt moments before.

****

A little after nine that evening, when the Previous Me would have been settling into a book or a radio program with the cat in my lap, I am instead phoning Uncle Charlie's so as to speak with an Army Air Corps pilot I met three days ago. Charlie answers, kids me about staying up past my bedtime, and then sets the receiver down while he fetches his nephew.

In that semi-silent space, when one is waiting on someone to pick up at the other end, the galaxy is full of possibility. If the science fiction writers are correct and parallel universes exist, then the doorway is somewhere in that gap in the telephone line.

The gap closes when Derek says, "This is either the colonel telling me that my leave's canceled early or a certain detective with a fondness for Kathy Mack's coffee."

"I'm not a detective."

"So you say."

"How are the hubcaps?"

"Numerous and well-sorted. Any luck?"

"I've written down the numbers of seventeen different filling stations, oil companies, and delivery services within city limits."

"Seventeen, huh? And you're planning on ringing them all?"

"Tomorrow morning, yes."

"And asking about the colors of their uniforms?"

"Do you have a better suggestion?"

"Would you say you're trying to *detect* the correct uniform color?"

I smile in spite of myself. "Fine. If I'm a detective,

99

what does that make you?"

"A detective's rickshaw driver? Look, kidding aside, I think it's time we start to proceed a bit more cautiously."

"What do you mean?"

He pauses for a moment, then says, "Let's say you locate those two men who tried to extort the refugees. They could be dangerous. Maybe more than you realize."

I readjust the telephone against my ear. "I hadn't thought about that." But Derek's right. If my unspoken hypothesis is that at least one of those men is guilty of Kaz's murder, perhaps in revenge for a broken nose courtesy of Kelly Mahone, then confronting him would not be wise. "What do you suggest?"

"Make your calls tomorrow. Don't give out your name. Let me know what you find."

"And then?"

"And then we'll see. I'm assuming at some point your plan is to go the police?"

"If I have anything worth reporting."

"Something tells me that we're getting closer to that point. The Agawa family chose the right person for this job."

"Maybe."

"Well, goodnight, Mrs. Maybe. I'll bring breakfast." He hangs up before I can reply.

****

On July 8, the front page of the *Star* features a photo of Howard Hughes's burning spy plane and a story about the cattle received in the local stockyards—a near record number, apparently. On page two is an ad that makes me produce a sound that is part laughter and part snort: *Pamper and pretty your neck with a strand of 14K gold* *beads—in two tones—back again after so long unattainable. $85. Price includes fed tax.*

Clearly I am reading the wrong newspaper.

I scan all twenty pages for any reference to refugees, warehouses, or the like. I find only one mention of anything remotely connected to the Japanese, this being a former Marine and POW, Bill Larson, who managed to argue his way out of a traffic ticket. According to the story, Larson weighed 170 pounds when he was captured at Wake Island and 83 when he was released—none of which is relevant either to the traffic stop or to my investigation.

And so I settle in with my pearl-colored telephone and seventeen businesses to call.

Here's my meager cover story: I work at Applegate's Laundry Service, and I'm asking about a lost-and-found item, a workingman's jacket in blue, with red stripes. And because I am now a para-professional liar, I seamlessly repeat this message every time the switchboard connects me to the next seven-digit number. Midway through this marathon, a knock at the door provides anticipated respite and I welcome Derek and his paperboard containers of hashbrowns and sausages from the diner. In between bites, I continue down the list, and when it's finally over, I have compiled these notes in my stenographer's book:

Company Name - R&B Uniforms?

1. Mansell Bros. - No

2. Flying "A" Station - No

And et cetera, all the way to number 17. When it's over, I draw a circle around the only two names with a possible match—Kroll and Sons Transport Company and Dougherty's Fuel and Fill.

"Aren't you afraid of what your neighbors might think?" Derek says.

I finish the last of my breakfast and wipe my mouth. "I don't understand."

Derek leans back in his chair, coffee in hand. Today he wears cap-toe shoes with two-tone laces. Because his trousers feature cuffs and pleats, I know they are a recent purchase, as those extras went away during the war, along with anything else seen as extraneous. He has hung his fedora on my coatrack by the door. "You're a single woman being visited at odd hours by a man from out of town."

"Oh, I see. In that case, no. My only neighbors are the Puerto Rican couple downstairs, and they're far too much in love with each other to waste any time thinking about the madwoman who lives in the attic. But I'm sure Nat Looper will have something to say about it."

"And he is?"

"Our resident vagrant and soothsayer. On most days he's found chatting up the customers outside the tobacconist's shop next door. He's harmless." I ignore the two circled names for a moment. "Why aren't you married?"

"That's an awfully direct question."

"I'm less discreet than I was four days ago."

"And why is that?"

"Four days ago, I was given enough money to pay my rent for the next two years."

"Thinking of quitting the telephone exchange?"

"I'm thinking that I don't need to be so concerned with discretion anymore."

"Liberated by your riches?" He smiles. "As it happens, I was engaged to be married once, but it didn't work out. She was a schoolteacher and an artist, with an Irish accent. Then the war rolled in, and I found myself wed to a beautiful lady called a P-51 Mustang. I'm sure things would have worked out differently, for me and everyone else in the world, if we hadn't been tearing one another to pieces for the last half-dozen years."

"What do you do in the Air Corps, now that the fighting is over?"

"Train young fools for whatever war comes next."

"Surely there can't be another, not like that."

"Every generation has its own."

After that bleak prediction, I'm not really sure what to do other than return to my list, but then something new occurs to me.

Derek sees it in my face. "What is it?"

"The Agawas paid me over nine hundred dollars."

"Yes, you could almost go out and purchase a new Chevrolet Stylemaster."

"Kaz worked as a custodian."

Derek rubs his smooth chin. "I see your point."

"His salary wouldn't have been any higher than mine. He was lucky to have a job at all, considering he was Japanese."

"Then where did his family get the money? What did they do before the war, before they were put in a camp? I know that a lot of the Japs had great jobs in San Francisco and places like that. Maybe the Agawas had savings stored away."

I have no answers for any of those questions because Kaz wasn't really my friend. I barely knew him. He was a pleasant man with whom I exchanged trivialities on certain mornings. This makes me feel like a heel. "More importantly," I say, steering the conversation away from my guilt, "I have a paper due tomorrow, so I need to spend some time with a typewriter this morning so as not to fail law school before I've really even gotten started."

"And those two businesses on your list?"

"We'll visit them in person this afternoon, if that's all right."

"Sounds swell, but what about the switchboard? Don't you work today?"

"Haven't you heard? A strange man brought me breakfast, and something in the sausage made me quite ill. I'm afraid I won't be able to sit on that stool for very long without becoming sick. Hopefully a trip to the pharmacist's will make things right again."

"Uh-huh. That money is already going to your head."

I toast him with the last sip of my coffee.

Chapter Fourteen

In Which I Roll Snake Eyes

Here is the thing about typewriters: they were invented by a lunatic.

I don't know his name. But as someone who struggles consistently to push the keys in the proper order, I am certain that only a drunk or a sadist would mix up the alphabet into the cipher that is the arrangement in front of me. All of the vowels are on the top line—except let's put the "A" down one row lower for no particular reason—and let's start the layout with "Q" because it's one of the least-used letters so it needs to be featured prominently instead of being stuck down there with "Z" and "X" where it belongs.

That is to say, my typing skill is not my finest feature.

Nevertheless, I complete my assignment a little after the lunch hour and slide it into a large envelope I'll deliver to my professor's office on Holmes Street, along with other artifacts of my collegiate life, including abstracts of court decisions and personal reflections on such cases as *Plessy v. Ferguson* and the Dred Scott decision.

I tap my finger on the envelope. Given recent events, I might steer my research toward *Korematsu v. the United States.* In that decision, handed down in 1944, the

Supreme Court declared that the government had the right to incarcerate Americans of Japanese descent, in the interest of national security. Even in its ruling that affirmed President Roosevelt's executive order, the Court admitted that a certain group was being denied its Constitutional rights. Yet the justices still permitted the imprisonment of over one hundred thousand innocent people.

I'm not yet a lawyer, but that contradiction sounds like bullshit to me—pardon the Français.

****

"Good Monday to you, Mrs. Frisco," Nat says as when I emerge at noon, envelope in one hand, handbag in the other. He mans his post beside the wooden statue, his beard showing a bit of gray. "Off to work, are ya?"

"Something like that. Here." I extend a five-dollar bill.

Nat beholds this offering solemnly. His watery eyes move from my hand to my face. "You sure about that, ma'am?" It's more than a day's wages.

"Will you spend it with wisdom and prudence?"

He cracks a grin. "I make no promises I can't keep."

"Fair enough."

He takes the money. "The blessings of the saints upon you."

"And upon you." I wave at Derek, who waits at the curb.

****

Kansas City is split in half. Cross the river, and you change states. Kroll and Sons Transport Company is located on the Kansas side, one block north of the Blind Institute. The large sign on the front of the Kroll building features three caricatures of dogs, one of them driving a

106

truck while the other two struggle to hang on.

Derek slows the car. "Strategy?"

"I believe you Air Corps chaps would call it long-range reconnaissance."

"Roger that." He stops far enough away that we can observe without being noticed. The Cord is as conspicuous as a colt among cows.

I make a shelf of my hand and place it above my eyes to thwart the afternoon sun. It's eighty-five degrees and climbing. Trucks with three axles wait in a dirt lot. One is a flatbed. The others are box trucks with the faded company logo painted on the sides.

"Pre-war vehicles," Derek observes, his eyes properly shaded by the rim of his fedora. "Look like Internationals, probably ten years old, at least. They've seen better days."

"Haven't we all?" I stare at the building's main door, waiting for someone to emerge.

"I suppose we're looking for a man with a busted nose?"

"Could we be so lucky?"

"Uncle Chuck carries a rabbit's foot in his pocket."

"I didn't know that. Does it help?"

"He says the one day he forgot and left it at home, he had a blowout at the Johnson County line and nearly crashed into a windmill. So there's your proof."

The door opens. Two men emerge. They both wear blue uniforms with red piping—the very colors that Jesse Imada described.

I sit up straighter, squinting.

"Those aren't exactly jackets," Derek says.

It's true. The men wear workman's coveralls, deep blue, with a vertical red band up the legs. One them gestures at a joke and the other laughs.

When I conducted my false survey for a business that does not actually employ me, Kroll and Sons answered that their workers wear blue with red. That much is accurate, but these baggy coveralls with the buttons up the front are likely not the garment in question. "This isn't the place. Can we try the other one?"

"Of course." He ignites the Cord's engine.

Dougherty's Fuel and Fill is strategically positioned at the stockyards, which straddle the state border at the place where the Kansas River almost touches Genessee Street. The Kansas Pacific and Missouri Pacific rails converge here, along with almost a dozen smaller lines, a nexus of loading docks and livestock pens, crammed with thousands of cattle. On a calm and windless day, the smell is almost philosophical in its power.

We pull into the filling station. Within moments, an attendant in a peaked cap hustles toward us, smiling like a magazine advertisement for dental care. He asks Derek about his fuel preference and an oil check, while I study his attire. He wears blue with red stripes, but in the form of a vest with multiple tool pockets. Beneath the vest is a white shirt with the filling-station star on the sleeve.

As he speaks with the attendant, Derek gives me a quick glance. I shake my head.

We fill up with fuel. At twenty-one cents a gallon, this costs me three dollars, as I have insisted on paying. This is followed by a brief discussion of the weather—a little rain could really cool things off—and then we pull away, veering from the odor and then idling at a stop sign while a slow-moving bus crosses the intersection.

Hand on the gearstick, Derek says, "Looks like we

shot craps."

"I'm not sure I know what that means."

"Oh, a silly dice game that men play because we're fools. The goal is to roll the correct number before you roll the wrong one."

"I believe I saw that in *Casablanca*."

"Exactly. And if you throw two sixes it's called a boxcar, and you lose. The same goes for two ones. That's called snake eyes. I believe that a roll of three is also a loss. At any rate, losing the wager is known as crapping out."

"Yes, it would seem we have." I drum my fingers against the car, my arm draped over the door. I was so certain of my clever research with the telephone index that I feel like pouting, as silly as that may be. The two men who possibly murdered Kaz are out there somewhere, one of them wearing that damned jacket, and now they will likely remain anonymous. At some point, I will need to admit defeat.

As the bus finally gets out of the way, I wonder aloud, "What do we do now?"

"How about a late lunch or an early dinner?"

"You're hungry? It's not even three in the afternoon."

"In the military, if you're not fighting or training, you're sleeping or eating."

"What do you suggest?"

"Our favorite spot."

"Do we have a favorite spot?"

"How soon she forgets." We zing down the street.

Kathy Mack's diner is somewhat controversial. The door for the white folks is directly adjacent to the door for the black folks. This allows the restaurant to meet city ordinance—the letter of the law—but not precisely in a manner agreeable to everyone—a subtle thumbing of the nose at the spirit of the law. The building is shaped like an L, with the white service along one leg and the colored service along the other. Caucasian waitresses and Negro waitresses work from the same kitchen but never cross the invisible Maginot Line between the two dining areas. According to local legend, Kathy Mack herself, a woman as white as ivory, had a Creole lover in the days of her wild youth, and the torch still burns. The side-by-side doors represent her soft spot for people of the darker race. Or so they say.

"I'm thinking sautéed chicken livers," Derek says from somewhere behind his menu.

"Baked ham sandwich?" It occurred to me about two and a half minutes ago that I have not sat across from a man at a meal since the night before Jim enlisted—not counting the coffee and Danish roll I sometimes eat while taking notes across Corky Schneider's desk. "The tomato soup sounds tempting, but probably the ham."

The radio on the counter plays a swing number as a waitress named Pauline places two bottles of Dr. Pepper on our table, bubbles fizzing to the top.

Derek gives her our order, and as Pauline departs, he says, "So tell me about these Monarchs of yours."

"What about them?"

"Are they any good?"

"They're leading the league, and Willard Brown is batting over three hundred."

"Why the fascination?"

"The two Minor League teams here both play in Blues Stadium, which is close to where I grew up. Watching the games was something to do when you were a girl who didn't make friends easily."

"I don't think I've ever met a woman who follows baseball."

"Well, *follow* isn't quite what I do. I haven't attended a game in years. But the papers print the box scores. The only thing I follow these days are men in blue-and-red jackets, but that doesn't seem to be working out."

"What's our next move?"

"I'm considering crying into my ham sandwich." I try a smile on for size, find that my heart isn't in it, and follow it with a sigh. "Honestly, my move should be returning Mrs. Agawa's money. I haven't helped at all."

"Have you thought any more about where they could have gotten that kind of cash?"

"I assume Kaz wasn't always a custodian. I have no idea what he did before the internment camps. He might have owned a Rolls Royce, for all I know."

"Could you talk to his wife?"

"Thought about it. But the next time she sees me, she'll be expecting answers."

"What, then?"

"Maybe Corky knows something about him."

"The fellow I met at the barbecue?"

"The one and the same."

"How does he figure into this?"

"He has an office in the building where Kaz died. They knew each other. Corky was the one who found the body." I give Derek a sanitized version of my recent past, scrubbed mostly clean of emotion, and by the time I'm finished, the food has arrived to save me.

As he eats, Derek says, "Uncle Chuck filled me in on some of that."

"On the details of my life?"

"He didn't go into specifics."

"What about you?"

"Me?" He pauses for a moment with his knife and fork above his chicken livers. "Other than occasionally flying a plane at four hundred miles an hour, I lead a boring life, at least up until a few days ago when I volunteered to drive you to a funeral."

"What did you do before?"

He doesn't have to ask me to define *before*. Everyone lived a life prior to Pearl Harbor that was different than it is today. "I was destined to be an auto mechanic, like many of the other esteemed men in my family. If you want the embarrassing truth, I had a dream of moving to Indianapolis and owning a racing team. Once I was in the Air Corps, the auto mechanic quickly became an aircraft mechanic, and they must have been desperate to catch up to the *Luftwaffe*, because they talked the mechanic into becoming a pilot. Are you considering dessert?"

I already eyed the chocolate ice cream on the menu. "Maybe. And you golf?"

"Poorly. But I suppose it's the closest thing I have to a hobby."

I have more questions for him but hold my tongue. I am having an actual conversation with an actual man, and if there's one thing they tell you in the ladies' magazines, it's to let him steer the conversation.

But he drives it right back to me. "What happens next with the investigation?"

"Are we still calling it that?"

"You're keeping a notebook, making telephone calls, and surveilling people from across the street. Do you have a better name for it?"

I lean back in the booth, its red cushion uneven from years of use. "We go to Corky's office, the place where Kaz was killed."

"I'm in." Derek hoists his bottle of soda.

I do the same. "To not crapping out."

"Agreed." He smiles. We touch bottles and drink at the same time.

Chapter Fifteen

In Which I Take a Detour

The bloodstain has been cleaned from the floor. I don't know how they've done it so successfully. Somewhere, a cleaning product is missing out on a fine opportunity to advertise to housewives across America its ability to *Remove All Trace of Murder—Fast!* This bit of black humor rises in me without bidding, perhaps an attempt to normalize the dread.

"Are you all right?" Derek asks.

"Not at all." It's as if Kaz were never here.

The lobby contains little of note. Nevertheless, I survey it with interest, looking for anything that didn't matter before but matters now.

My surname used to be printed on the office door, so I've never knocked before entering. I find Corky with one hand in his hair and the other turning the pages of a legal treatise. He looks up and seems relieved to have a break. He closes the book. We say our hellos, and he stands when he sees Derek and then makes a gesture that asks us to dismiss the clutter.

"O'Brien, isn't it?" Corky asks.

"That's right." They shake in that solid, timeless way that men have of doing it, like they might either be fast friends or dueling with pistols at dawn a week from now.

We seat ourselves at Corky's invitation. He indicates the liquor cabinet, if either of us is interested. Derek accepts. Corky has let the office go a bit since my last visit, folders stacked out of order, the wastebasket full. I suppose no one has been hired since Kaz to keep things up. On the desk, Betty and David Niven smile at me, the housewife just as glamorous as the movie star.

"Surprised to see you this hour of day," Corky says. "No shift this afternoon?"

"I'm sure they'll be fine without me. Is this a good time?"

"Not really, to be honest. Between the telephone and the typewriter, it's a miracle I can get anything done. You should hurry up and get that degree so I can make you a junior partner."

"Business is good?"

"Steady but boring until recently." He stares at his packet of cigarettes without extracting one, as if gripped by a sudden thought. A fan on the open windowsill pushes warm air around the room. Corky's eyes move to me and then to Derek before fixing on his matchbook. He lights up, exhales, and says, "You're here about Agawa, aren't you?"

"Actually, yes."

"You find anything at the building I told you about, the one on Benton Street?"

"I haven't uncovered the identity of the murderer, if that's what you're asking. I wanted to talk to you about your relationship with him."

"With Agawa? Wasn't much of a relationship. We chatted on most mornings. Nice fella. But I don't think I ever saw him outside of work."

"You wouldn't mind answering a few questions?

There's a chance he could have said something about his home life, his hobbies—"

"Yeah, sure, no problem. Listen, I have a new client that pays well, as in the kind of money those suits over at Covey and Bryant are making."

"Sounds wonderful."

"I agree, and it *was* wonderful, but now I'm not so sure. I really want to do right by this guy, on account of what I'm billing him an hour, but the case against him is pretty tight. Maybe that's somewhere you could help. I'm lucky you stopped by." He taps his finger on his desk blotter, never looking away from me. "Yeah, that just might be the ticket to fixing this."

"Fixing what?" And then I remember, one week ago, I was leaving Corky's office and sensed that something wasn't quite right with him. "What's the situation?"

Corky takes a drag, then rests his cigarette on the rim of the ceramic ashtray so he can lean forward, elbows on his desk, his tie loose at his throat. "There are certain parts of this story that aren't protected by the legal agreement with my client, so I can sketch the basics for you. I'm needing a particular piece of research completed to help exonerate my client, but so far I've hit a dead end."

"Just tell me what you'd like me to do."

"Okay, this goes back to before the war, when the Pendergrast Machine and all the other political unions were pulling the strings."

Derek has poured a whiskey from Corky's modest cabinet. He gives it a swirl around his glass. "Pardon a guy from out of town, but what's the Pendergrast Machine?"

"Used to be a big player in politics," Corky explains, "all the way from the turn of the century to just a few years back. The Pendergrast folks had the muscle to get their men into all the important city offices, and they made a point of sharing the spoils with the locals."

"The Robin Hood effect," I say.

"Exactly. In the end, though, it was all about power and money, like it always is. They got Truman elected to the senate, and look where that ended up—the Oval Office."

"But they're gone now?" Derek asks.

"For the most part, yes. Prosecutors ended up with something like three hundred Pendergrast people behind bars. Not a single person was acquitted. That was ten years ago, at least. Things are different now. The state commission pays a lot closer attention to the operations of the county boards, which brings me to my client, who's been charged with election fraud. They say he illegally registered voters."

"Not an uncommon practice back then," I note. As Corky said, since the '30s, players in the big political gangs have been indicted in droves as part of a government crackdown.

"My client says the ballot box was indeed rigged, but not by him. He's forced to keep his mouth shut."

"Forced how?"

"On threat of his life, I suppose."

"By whom?"

"I can't tell you that, sorry."

"Is he telling the truth?"

"You're the future lawyer. You tell me."

"Fine. It doesn't matter if it's true. It's your job to convince a jury that he isn't guilty."

"Right-o. But to do that, I'll need more than just his word. It's easy to blame the bogeyman, but unless you have a witness to corroborate the story, the bogeyman gets off scot-free."

"And you have such a witness?"

"Maybe. My client says that a woman named Helena Crenshaw can substantiate the facts, so I need her to testify on his behalf."

"Where do I come in?"

"As it turns out, Helena Crenshaw is not only a socialite with a lot of important friends, but her family operates a good portion of the city's bookmaking business. Horses, mainly, but any kind of sports betting probably goes through one of her extended family members. She has a lot of influence in this town, and that would count for something on the witness stand."

"I don't know anything about horse races." In fact, that entire side of Kansas City—the side that until the war was operated by criminals—is so far removed from my daily life that it might as well be situated in Sicily. "Why can't you just pay this person a visit and ask if she'll help your client?"

"Easier said than done. I tried telephoning her. She doesn't take calls from attorneys with clients being investigated by the government. Go figure. I guess the professional bookies don't like lawyers any more than they like federal agents. No one there will talk to me. So I'm asking you to meet with her. I'll give you enough details about the case that you can lay it out for her and hopefully get her on board. She won't shut the door on you."

"How can you be so sure?"

"Because"—he waves his hand vaguely— "because

you have a nice face."

"Thank you, but that hardly guarantees I'll get a meeting with her."

"I think maybe it does, in this case."

"I don't understand. What are you trying to say?"

Corky goes back to his cigarette. "She's a dame who likes other dames, okay?"

"Ms. Crenshaw is a lesbian."

"Jesus, Viv, yes, all right, she is. Can you work with that or not?"

"I'm not sure I know what you mean."

"You're enjoying my discomfort, aren't you? Look, do this for me right now, and I'll help out with Agawa any way I can. I'll recite from memory every single word I ever exchanged with the man. And I'll sweeten the deal by paying you ten bucks. How does that sound?"

"Ten dollars?" I glance at Derek. "It's a bit less than my usual fee."

He nods. "A little."

"Viv, please."

"Yes, Corky, of course. We'll do what we can." It would take me two days at the switchboard to earn ten dollars. I could get used to this.

****

Corky cannot divulge his client's identity until I become his assistant, so I sign my name to a hastily typed contract, and just like that, I am a professional. It may not be entirely proper, but if I'm able to secure Ms. Crenshaw's testimony, the client certainly won't complain.

That client is one Oliver R. Bishop, election director of Jackson County. He's been charged with fraud, allegedly altering election rolls for the sake of tipping a hotly contested city council seat in favor of a candidate supporting pari-mutuel betting.

"May I ask you something unrelated to any of this?" Derek says over the Cord's engine.

"Of course."

"Have you ever driven an automobile?"

"On a public road? No. In a cow pasture, yes."

"How long ago was that?"

"If you're thinking of inviting me to take the wheel, I'll forevermore consider you highly untrustworthy."

He laughs.

"Besides," I continue, "why should I have any interest in driving when the view from the passenger's seat is so panoramic?"

We traverse the city with the top down and the summer sun in our eyes. I provide the navigation—"Turn here, go there"—as I am the native guide. I have lived on the Missouri-Kansas border all my life. What I lack in worldliness I make up for nicely in local expertise—whatever that's worth. We eventually find our way to 19th Street, just across from Club Mardi Gras, where even at this hour of early evening, musicians have gathered on the walk outside for an improvised jazz set.

As Derek brings the car to a slow stop, I ask him, "What would you have called this racing team of yours?"

"Pardon?"

"You said you wanted to move to Indianapolis and launch a racing outfit."

"Ah. The dreams of a boy. But I suppose I would have called us something unimaginative like O'Brien Motorsports."

"You're right. Unimaginative."

"What would you have suggested?"

"Let me think about it. Is this the place?"

The building's roof projects out over the avenue, with scrolling woodwork from a bygone age. Layers of paint hold the cornices together. The façade is mostly windows, the glass painted with a cool frost so that I can't quite see inside as I close the Cord's door and approach, adjusting my hat. I'm sweating lightly. The fellow on the bass across the street plucks a steady, heavy note that tugs at me like an undercurrent at sea.

"Have you ever heard of this person?" Derek asks.

"Ms. Crenshaw? Not at all."

"What's our angle here? How do we approach her?"

"Would you be morally opposed to me telling her the truth?"

"I suppose there's a time and place for honesty."

We stop before a door printed with a woefully uninspiring name: Family Investment Capital.

I give him a sideways glance. "How about Derek's Dynamos?"

He makes a cringey face.

"Right. Maybe not." I try the door. Though I half-expect the place to be closed for business at this hour, the door opens onto a room that looks like those photographs you see of the New York Stock Exchange after a busy day of trading—the people are gone, but the disarray remains. A wall-length blackboard is covered in numbers and names. A spiral staircase made of wrought iron ascends to a second-floor balcony. Voices drift down from above.

"Hello?" I step inside, Derek behind me.

The source of the room's papery mess is an object I identify on sight: a teleprinter. From my training at the switchboard, I understand the basic operation of such a machine, this one being a Creed, Model 6 or perhaps 7, capable of printing about sixty-five words per minute. The Telex network connects most of North America and allows an operator to relay messages to a receiver thousands of miles away. I use one occasionally at work.

"Hello, is anyone here?"

A man appears at the railing above. His white shirt is partially unbuttoned, his sleeves rolled up. Such is the lax business attire of every man in town these days; it's simply too hot to be buttoned down. "Sorry, folks, we're closed. Come see us in the morning."

"Is Ms. Crenshaw available?"

"Like I said, come back tomorrow."

"We're here regarding Mr. Oliver Bishop."

He stares down at me for a moment more, then turns and disappears into an upstairs room.

While we wait, I say, "How about O'Brien's Automotive Adventurers?"

"Are you going to keep this up all evening?"

"You don't like the name?"

"Do you have anything shorter?"

"O'Brien's Autos?"

"That sounds as if I sell used cars."

"Fair enough."

The man reemerges on the balcony and points to a church pew that has been converted into a waiting area near one of the many desks. "Hang tight."

We follow his instructions. The lights in this spacious room have been turned off, so the illumination is provided by the setting sun, which streams through the frosted glass and renders triangular shadows on the floor. Across the street, the jazz players are picking up speed, though I can't quite make out the melody from here.

For a moment, just one thin moment, I marvel at what I'm doing, sitting here, putting my nose where it doesn't precisely belong. Who have I become?

Helena Crenshaw appears at the top of the stairs. She looks like she's practiced that pose in that particular place. She wears a fitted bolero jacket over a long green skirt. She would be easy to envy for her cascade of red hair, given the general lifelessness of my own.

"I'm told you're here about Oliver?"

I stand up as she descends. "Yes, ma'am."

She takes her time. Every revolution around the winding stairs is a second of suspense that I suspect she enjoys. I've known women like that, the *enjoyers*, the ones who seem to find the rest of us amusing. My patience expires by the time she reaches the floor. I introduce myself and my associate, mention our alliance with a certain local law firm, and thank her for taking the time to meet with us.

Ms. Crenshaw offers Derek one version of a smile and me a different one, then tips her head in the direction of the music from the club. "Best thing about this location is being serenaded every evening, wouldn't you say?"

"The music's nice. Do you mind answering a few questions?"

"You're lawyers?"

"Neither one of us, actually. I work for Mr. Schneider."

"His secretary?"

"His assistant."

"Why haven't we met before, you and I?"

"I guess I don't have a very wide social circle."

"Then it must be my lucky day. Of course, you know

I can't vouch for Oliver in his current legal predicament."

"And why is that?"

"Because the bastard shot my horse."

"I beg your pardon?"

She smiles. She's older than I first thought. "We better sit down, the three of us. It's past the close of the business day, and I'm done standing up for a while." She moves toward an office, the path between here and there littered with discarded teleprinter pages. "What was it that the spider said to the fly?" She motions us inside.

Chapter Sixteen

In Which I Make a Bet

You will play so often in the sun that your shadow will never be lonely.

So I was told when I was twelve. That prophecy returns to me now as my shadow reaches across the parquet floor in the direction of Helena Crenshaw. She has removed her jacket and sits bare-shouldered on a chaise that looks out of place in an office that is otherwise monkish and masculine. Derek and I occupy wretched metal chairs.

"I don't let just anybody in after hours, you understand," she says.

"What is it that you do here exactly?"

"You don't know?"

"From what I've heard, your company processes legal wagers."

"Legal now, yes, but it didn't used to be that way. These days we're national, thanks to technology. They can't build those telephone lines fast enough, if you ask me. Are you familiar with how the betting system works?"

"Is this related to Mr. Bishop's predicament?"

"Indirectly."

I move my hand in a way that invites her to proceed. She leans back on her sofa. "There are two types of betting systems, fixed-odds and pari-mutuel. The first one is rather straightforward. Let's say a sporting event takes place on Saturday. On Tuesday, you come see me and place a bet on the outcome of that event. We lock in your odds and shake on it, so to speak. No matter what happens between Tuesday and Saturday, your odds stay the same, and so does your potential payout."

"So…if I were to bet on the Monarchs winning that Saturday game, but on Thursday our best hitter got injured…"

"Nothing would change for you, because you'd placed your bet before the injury. Now, if a fellow came to me on Thursday, I'd give him a very different set of odds on that game."

"I understand."

"The house gets the same take, regardless. We put a commission on every bet. It's called a vigorish. Basically, you pay me for the opportunity to win or lose."

"And pari-mutuel?"

"The odds move up and down all the way to the moment of the event, depending on the number of bettors and the amount they've wagered. In racing, that means a horse could potentially earn you five hundred dollars when you enter your bet on Tuesday but pays out only fifty when it wins on Saturday night."

"So the more people who think the horse is going to win, the more its odds improve, and the less money everyone makes."

She nods.

"And if no one thinks the horse stands a chance—"

"That's what we call a longshot."

"And if the horse wins anyway?"

"Then someone stands to make a king's ransom."

"And how is Oliver Bishop in trouble over this?"

"Dear old Ollie is accused of helping to ensure that the city voted in favor of legalizing the pari-mutuel style of gambling. Prior to the war, the racket was operated strictly under the table."

"Did Mr. Bishop stuff the ballot box?"

"That's for a jury to decide."

"I was told you could provide evidence to exonerate him."

"And you're here to convince me to help?"

"Is it true? Is he innocent?"

"Far from innocent, I assure you. And we're not precisely on speaking terms, he and I. Oliver has always dabbled in racing. He's bought and sold a few horses, tried his hand at training—found it all far more glamorous than he thought it would be. After all, we aren't exactly the Kentucky Derby around here."

"So what happened? What went wrong?"

Helena lets out a small sound, something between a sigh and a whistle. "Tell you what. Come back in the morning and we'll chat like old friends, just the two of us. All the cards on the table."

Her omission of Derek in this invitation isn't lost on me. "What's wrong with now?"

"Our little shop is closed for the day, dearie. I'm tired, and it's time for a drink. The sun is over the yardarm, as they say." Before I can propose a counter offer, she gets to her feet. "Breakfast is served at nine. We work while we eat around here, so do try to keep up."

Before I know it, Derek and I are back on the sidewalk. Across the street, the musicians that a poet once called long-headed jazzers play a number that transforms sunset into night.

****

On Tuesday, July 9, a miracle happens.

It rains.

At first I'm not sure what's awakened me. Satchel is the usual culprit, a repeat offender when it comes to dragging me from a beautifully dreamless sleep. But it's not the cat. I open my eyes. Water runs down the window in silver threads.

I rise. My bare feet carry me closer. The rain is overdue. The city has been slowly baking. Every week it seems that another green place has been replaced with concrete as we rush away from the war that ended less than a year ago and toward what President Truman promises to be prosperity. Sometimes I believe him.

With the windows now open to let in the shower's scent, I face the firing squad of my wardrobe. To earn Corky's promised payment, I'll need to convince Helena Crenshaw, bookmaker and socialite, that her testimony is necessary. If this were a job interview, what would I wear? What *could* I wear, given the state of affairs in my closet?

I still own nothing with pockets or pleats. No one sold skirts like that during the war, because it meant excess fabric that was better used elsewhere. In the shop windows downtown, such designs are rushing back. Excess is fashionable again. Maybe I'll reward myself, when all of this is done.

Until then, I choose a yellow blouse with a Peter Pan neckline and a jacket with wide lapels and sharp points. I add a matching skirt, and my favorite hat, but please do not get me started on my lack of cosmopolitan shoes.

Derek picks me up at twenty minutes till nine.

"You'll be fine today?" he asks as he holds open the

Cord's door, shielding me with an umbrella.

"Without my partner in crime, you mean?"

"Well, I haven't done much so far but glower at witnesses."

I get in. He shuts the door. I watch him walk around the car, folding the umbrella as he goes, a man who doesn't seem to mind the rain on his face.

As he settles in behind the wheel, I say, "What plans do you have today?"

He indicates his golf cap. "A retired colonel I know lives down in Topeka. He says he's up for at least nine holes. The news announcer says the rain isn't likely to last."

"The radio is predicting the weather now?"

"Not with much accuracy, I'm afraid."

"If I remember correctly, rain or shine, your leave expires in ten days."

"Think you'll wrap this up by then?"

"Frankly, I'm not even sure what *this* is. But I hope so."

"Are you going in to work this afternoon or opting for truancy?"

"I've not yet decided. What do you recommend?"

"That's up to you. Either way, you'll need a ride from Ms. Crenshaw's when you're finished there."

"I'll come up with something."

"Yes, I suppose you did find your way around town long before I showed up."

"Nevertheless, thank you for answering the summons."

He fires up the engine. It starts on the first try. "What can I say? I'm a military man. If there's one thing I'm good at, it's following orders."

"I prefer to think of them as requests."

He laughs, the sound loud within the small space of the car, and I sit here under a rainy roof and enjoy the feeling of the smile on my face.

****

What happens upon my arrival at Ms. Crenshaw's bookmaking company is, chronologically, this:

1. Dappled in raindrops, I enter the messy workroom floor.

2. Three men with telephone receivers under their chins hardly pay me a glance.

3. Ms. Crenshaw, dressed in trousers, smiles and bids me to follow her.

4. Wisps of *Moment Volé* perfume lead me past the rattling teleprinter.

5. I ask Ms. Crenshaw what soured her relationship with Oliver Bishop.

6. She says, "Call me Helena," and presents a breakfast of honey biscuits and coffee.

7. Helena indicates a blackboard on the wall.

8. I see the names of the horses in the morning line, and she invites me to pick one.

9. Feeling game and weirdly sure of myself, I choose Run For Thunder.

10. Helena points out that my horse has 9/2 odds.

11. I ask if she's taking my five dollars or not.

12. She laughs, as leisurely as a woman in a hammock, then wonders about Derek.

13. I hand over my wager and inform her that Derek is my business partner.

14. Her eyes fall to my left hand.

15. So do mine. Resting there is an almost inconspicuous wedding band.

16. Seeing my face, Helena asks what happened.

17. I tell her that he died. I realize it's the first time in months I've said it out loud.

18. She opens her mouth to start with the I'm sorrys.

19. I cut her off and request that she simply tell me about Bishop.

20. She holds my stare, then sighs and looks away. "All right. You win."

****

"What you're about to hear is the truth," she begins, legs tucked under her, shoes on the floor, "though I'm not necessarily committed to repeating the story in court."

Notebook open in front of me, I simply nod.

"I met Ollie at a time in my life when I needed him most, I suppose."

"And when was that?"

"In my wayward youth I wasn't as circumspect as I should have been. But who knows anything about discretion when you're young? Who has time for it? At any rate, I was arrested for being suspected of violating the state's sodomy laws. I assume that I don't need to explain any further?"

Though I'm only a lawyer in training, I understand the legislation. It's forbidden by statute for two people of the same gender to engage in physical relations. But it happens. Scandals are increasingly common. "I'm sorry to hear that."

"Yes, well, the district attorney tends to go softer when it's two women involved than when it's two men, so after a proper scolding behind closed doors, they cut me loose without pressing charges. Still, though, it made the paper. I was *persona non grata* after that, but then

Germany bombed the hell out of Wieluń, and suddenly everyone was more concerned with Poland than they were with my recent sins. The war gave me the chance to turn things around. I inherited a business, turned it legitimate, and made a profit."

"The American dream?"

"To a T, my dear."

"And when does Mr. Bishop enter the picture?"

"He saw an opening, and I needed political support. We were both down-on-our-luck types, like a couple of railroad tramps, I suppose. We traded a series of favors that allowed us to drag ourselves up by our shared bootstraps, you might say. Ollie aspired to get rich as a racehorse owner or perhaps as a trainer—he never could decide quite which. He hit his big break when he convinced a famous jockey named Horace Brent to quit a million-dollar stable in Lexington and sign with him, instead. It was quite a coup, actually."

"I'm guessing it somehow didn't work out."

"And I was to blame, yes. Horace and his wife packed up everything and moved here. She was a Finnish immigrant named Marikka. She'd been a member of Finland's ski team in the Olympics in Bavaria. Without her mountains, she was positively lost here in the Midwest."

"I think I understand."

"Do you?"

"The two of you had an affair."

For a moment the only sound is the rain on the building's metal roof. Eventually Ms. Crenshaw says, "Very perceptive."

"You said yesterday that Mr. Bishop shot your horse?"

"In revenge, yes. You see, Horace Brent departed in a rage when Mari and I were silly enough to get ourselves caught. He quit the entire scene. Ollie never heard from him again. So he took a deer rifle and managed not to shoot his own foot off in the process of killing my best mare. I didn't think the idiot even knew one end of a gun from the other."

I continue to hold the notebook but haven't written down a single thing. "So you're not willing to give a statement on the idiot's behalf?"

"What's in it for me?"

"I don't think I have anything to offer."

"Everyone has something to offer."

I tilt my head, trying to guess. "What did you have in mind?"

"Meet me here tomorrow afternoon, twelve-thirty sharp. We'll take a road trip."

"And where is it that we're going on this excursion, exactly?"

She drains the last of her coffee like it's a shot of whiskey. "Have you ever been to the races?"

Chapter Seventeen

In Which I Negotiate a Deal

Ms. Peele knows something is going on.

The girls say she is formidable at cribbage. I've never seen her outside of work. She is impossible to envision in a social setting. I imagine she doesn't exist when I'm not here, like a character in a closed book. But they also say something else about Ms. Peele: she was a WAC officer who served in the Corps of Engineers somewhere in the desert of New Mexico, where they cracked the atom. We all have our pasts.

I am farther removed from mine than ever. I plug cables into the wall for hours, but I'm not really here. Instead I'm sitting in front of a captured Nazi flag. I'm having tea with evicted Japanese families in a riverside warehouse. I'm working the corner at a boxing match. I'm doing all of those things that I have no business doing, all because a kind man was killed.

Ms. Peele keeps glancing at me. I'm not quite bold enough to wink at her.

****

From my kitchen that night, using a number copied from the index when Ms. Peele was in the ladies' room, I ask the operator to connect me to the only listing for Agawa in the greater Kansas City area.

Time to report.

I've rehearsed my lines, but preparation doesn't settle my nerves. Rain streaks the kitchen window; it's been drizzling lightly all day. They say it falls on the just and the unjust alike.

A voice answers on the fourth ring.

I rush out my name and the reason for my call, and then I wait.

After a few seconds, Hiroto Agawa says, "It is good to hear from you, Vivian-san."

The last time I met Kaz's son, he was handing me an envelope of cash. Has his money been well spent? "Is this a good time to talk?" I ask. "I can telephone at a later time, if you want."

"Please, of course. Tell me what you've discovered." He briefly covers the receiver; I hear muffled Japanese. "We are very anxious to know."

I follow my script. Hiroto receives a step-by-step summary of everything I've done, everyone I've met, and everything I've learned. When I'm finished, I expect him to ask, *Is that all you've managed to accomplish?*

Instead he says only, "You have been very thorough."

"Not thorough enough. I don't have the answer for you yet."

"All things in their time."

"I hope so. I'll do my best to give you some closure." What was it that Ace said to me all those years ago on his parents' porch? *The best people in the world are the ones who don't let go.* "I'll ring you again as soon as I know more."

"Of course. *Domo arigato.*"

"You're welcome." And then he's gone, his faith in me reverberating in his wake. Or maybe it's merely politeness masquerading as faith.

I return the receiver to its cradle. Satchel slides onto my lap, requesting attention.

I console him absentmindedly and listen to the rain.

****

The precipitation stopped at some point in the middle of the night. I slept through the sky's quiet transition from clouds to stars. My dreams were fragments that I remembered perfectly upon waking but now, an hour later on the curb on a clear Wednesday morning, I can't remember at all.

I hear the Cord coming before it arrives. With a goodbye wave to Nat Looper at his post by the cigar-selling Indian, I open the passenger's door before Derek has a chance to get out and be chivalrous on my behalf.

He skips the good mornings and says, "So what happened yesterday after I dropped you off?"

"I bet on a horse."

"A winner, I hope?"

"I don't know. I didn't hear the result of the race. Probably not."

"And will Ms. Crenshaw provide a statement for your lawyer friend?"

"I think she and I are at the *quid pro quo* stage of our relationship."

"Meaning what? Did you promise her something in return?"

"Maybe. I'm not sure. I'm meeting her today at the track."

"What happens then?"

"Have you ever attended a horse race?"

"Sure, who hasn't? And greyhounds, once or twice."

"What do people wear? Is it formal?"

"What do they *wear*? Oh, I don't know. For men, a good blazer never goes out of style. I admit I'm relatively clueless when it comes to anything more complicated than that."

"Would you mind if we ran a few errands? I can pay for our fuel, if we're running low."

"Where are we going?"

"Somewhere dangerous."

"Is that so? And where might that be?"

"The department store."

"Ah. I better bring a helmet and my service pistol."

"At the very least." I can't help but smile at him. "Let's go shopping."

When in doubt, always begin with a new pair of shoes. For my first visit to the race track, I select a pair of lattice-front sandals with one-and-a-half-inch heels. For the dress, I settle on printed seersucker with a U-shaped neckline and a fully ruffled skirt. The total price is $8.98. While Derek browses men's haberdashery, I pay for my purchases with money I've not yet earned.

Buying new clothes is not my first indiscretion of the day. Before breakfast I telephoned the switchboard and lied with little hesitation. This is not a pattern I want to maintain, so I need to conclude my arrangement with the Agawas before I no longer have a job. What's more, Derek will depart on the eighteenth when his leave expires, so I can't afford to spend too much time enjoying myself like a debutante on her way to the ball. Still, though, it's nice to be frivolous for a change. I can't remember the last time.

Derek deposits me at Family Investment Capital a little after noon. Neighborhood boys earn their nickels by cleaning the flurry of paper scraps, receipts, and betting notes from the floor and depositing this refuse in large bins on the street corner. The city recently purchased a novel new truck called a Garwood Load Packer, complete with a compactor to compress the waste as the vehicle navigates the streets. It made the front page of the *Star* a few weeks back.

Helena Crenshaw is dressed as I imagine English cricket players dress, in a white short-sleeve top and matching pants that are as scandalous as she intends them to be, hugging her thighs and stopping three inches above the ankles. Her hat is broad enough to shield her complexion from the summer sun, complete with a plume.

I half expect her to greet me with a European kiss on either cheek, but she only waves her handbag and says, "We'll stop for lunch along the way, if you don't mind. I know a place." She doesn't break stride, leading me to the curb and slinging open the driver's door of a navy blue Cadillac coupe with a front grill so prominent it looks like a fence.

I'm barely settled in my seat before she starts the engine and pumps the gas pedal a few times, making an awful ruckus from the exhaust pipe.

"Sorry about that," she says. "I'm told it's the carburetor, or some such device."

"Couldn't prove it by me."

"You don't drive?"

"You're the second person to ask me that in recent days. Maybe I should learn."

"I earned the Automobiling Badge in the Girl Scouts when I was twelve, and I've never looked back." She gets us moving with a soft chirp of the tires.

And so we begin our escapade. I'm not at all sure

what to expect, but our conversation is lively and moves in a pleasing manner between unconnected topics. As we make our way out of town, the sun filling the sky, we talk about laundry detergent and state politics and the new motion picture releasing this week, the one with Gary Cooper, but neither of us can remember the title. We speak of our childhoods, our favorite desserts, and of course our love affairs—of which Helena has had many and I have had precisely one.

"You know, my personal heroine is Mata Hari," she says.

"The spy?"

"Did you hear that she blew the firing squad a kiss right before they shot her?"

"Sounds like a myth to me."

"More than a myth, dearie. A *legend*." She laughs and shifts the car into its next gear with only minimal trouble.

We arrive at the track half an hour later. If I am here to convince her to speak on Oliver Bishop's behalf, then I'll play my part, perhaps not with the *savoir faire* of Mata Hari, but hopefully enough to finish the job.

The first race is set to start within minutes. I bet on a horse named Showtime Sandy. We get to our seats just as the gates fly open. I surprise myself by putting my hands like a megaphone around my mouth and yelling at the silly thing to run faster, faster, faster.

****

Eleven races later, seven dollars lighter, I sit with my back to the sun and watch Helena sip her mint julep. Mine is already gone. As she finishes a story about the time she met Ernest Hemingway at a race in Chicago, I tilt my head in such a way that she understands the time has come. Over the last several hours I have held up my end of our patchwork agreement. My payment awaits.

She moves her fingertip around the rim of her glass. "So…"

"Mr. Schneider would like to know if he can count on you for a statement."

"Can your Mr. Schneider guarantee my safety?"

"Safety from what?"

"A few ballots were rigged that night. It's true. But not by Oliver. And don't ask me for a name because there are still men in this town who do business with shovels, if you know what I mean. I'll provide an alibi for Oliver, but only if my testimony is kept under wraps. If there's a chance my name could leak, I'm not your girl."

"What men are you talking about?"

"Play this game long enough, dearie, you're bound to find out."

"Fine. I suppose that doesn't matter at the moment. I'm sure everything can be arranged to keep your statement sealed. You'll do it, then?"

"That bastard still owes me a horse."

I pick up her cocktail and casually drink the last swallow. "I'll take that as a yes."

Chapter Eighteen

In Which My Luck Turns

If I have one regret about this afternoon, it's that I
didn't accept Helena's offer to drive. She pointed out a
perfectly good country road with empty prairie on either
side, not a bystander to be seen, innocent or otherwise.
But still I demurred, despite the sunshine, despite the
summer day. I respected my better judgment at the time,
though now I wonder why. Somewhere the poetess Edna
St. Vincent Millay is probably writing a sonnet about
women like me.

Our ride back from the racing track is pleasant. I
laugh at Helena's risqué jokes, and she convinces me to
admit aloud that my apartment is as exciting as a British
nunnery. She tells me that I need a night out on the town,
and I reply that I have forgotten what that means.

"Maybe it's just like riding a bike," she suggests.

"I haven't owned a bike since I was a girl."

"That's no excuse and you know it."

"Do I?" Of course I do, but I don't need to be
reminded of it.

It's funny: I've known the girls at the switchboard
for months, some even for years, and yet in all that time
I've not had a single conversation with one of them as
open and interesting as these few hours with Helena
Crenshaw. I'm climbing from her car, about to tell her as

much, when I stop and stare down the street.

There it is—a blue jacket with red stripes on the sleeves.

I freeze in place on the curb, a hand over my mouth. Two men drag cans across the pavement, hoist them up over their heads, and dump the contents into a compartment at the rear of the truck. These men wear the clothes described by the refugee Jesse Imada, their names stitched above the pockets on their chests.

"What is it, dearie? What's wrong?"

I take a few steps in that direction, shielding my eyes from the late-afternoon sun, trying to be sure.

"Vivian?"

"Sorry, it's just..." Giving Helena no further explanation, I approach the truck at a clip.

Is it safe?

I don't have time to consider an answer. "Excuse me, gentlemen."

One of them turns, his empty can rattling against the street. "Madam?"

"Where do you work?"

"Excuse me?" His face is ruddy, a cigarette hanging from his lower lip.

"Your employer?"

"Uh, the city, I guess."

"You guess?"

"No, ma'am. I mean, I get a paycheck from the city treasurer. Is something wrong?"

"Not at all." The suspects from the riverside warehouse, one of whom received a broken nose from Kelly Mahone, work for the same municipal waste-removal service as these men. "Thank you."

Just as Helena catches up, I take her elbow and rush

us both back to the car.

****

"I've lived in this city my entire adult life," Helena says, the setting sun in her eyes, "but I've never once been to the hole in the ground where they deposit my trash."

We sit in the Cadillac, engine off and ticking, across the street from a fenced area where men in matching uniforms offload residential waste. It is the evening of July 10, the temperature is at least ninety degrees, and though I am sweating in a most unladylike manner, I hardly notice.

"So you're saying one of these men murdered your friend?"

Am I saying that? I've given Helena a distilled version of my recent history.

She turns toward me. "Do I understand that correctly?"

"It's likely, yes."

"You're tracking a murderer?"

"I suppose you could say that."

After a moment, she smiles, showing her teeth. "My, my, dearie. You are full of—"

"Surprises, yeah, I know." I throw open my door and get out of the car.

****

A few minutes later, I watch as the foreman or manager or someone like that throws a bar across the gate and lights a pipe, signaling an end to the work day with a puff of smoke. He drops the match in the gutter. For the last half hour I've stood like a sentry nearby, scanning every face within range, looking for signs of Mahone's handiwork. No man with a bandaged face has emerged, though half a dozen have now departed, empty lunch pails swinging at their sides. Soon the foreman also clocks out, chugging away in an old car with a mostly flat rear tire. The sun sinks lower in the sky, and the street corner is quiet.

"So now what?" Helena asks. She's been marvelously patient through all of this.

"I try again tomorrow, I suppose."

"Try *what* again?"

"Observing. Waiting."

"I see. I'm starting to wonder what I've gotten myself into. Can I give you a ride home?"

Though home is the last place I want to be, this business must remain unfinished for now. A part of me wants to climb the fence and have a look around—which is a sure sign that I need a long, dreamless sleep. I accept Helena's offer. All the way across town she quizzes me on the case, and the fact that I'm now calling it a *case* means, one way or the other, I am committed to the end.

****

I phone Derek in the morning.

The first thing is he says is, "I've been wondering something."

"Wondering what?"

"If you're a law student, why don't you ever attend class?"

I tuck the receiver between my shoulder and chin so I can add notes from last night's surveillance to my stenographer's pad. "My current course meets twice a month and is primarily independent research. I found the red-and-blue jacket."

"You did?"

"Can you come over?"

"You located the men from the warehouse?"

"I need your help with that."

"You have it. I'll be there shortly."

He doesn't say goodbye before hanging up.

****

The human nose is comprised of nasal bones and maxillary bones. That's the breakable stuff, wedged in there among the protective cartilage. Without proper treatment, a broken nose can result in infection, a deviated septum, or even a brain fluid leak if the lining above the sinuses is cut. Healing time is generally three weeks. Armed with this knowledge from the encyclopedia and fortified by Kathy Mack's coffee, I lean against the Cord's fender, a mere twenty-two feet from the entry to the city's waste-disposal service.

"Think I'll visit the barbershop later," Derek says from his place beside me, "unless of course we're chasing a murderer down the street by then."

I glance at him. "You haven't a hair out of place."

"Well, you and Major Stanborne obviously have different opinions on personal grooming standards."

"He's that bad?"

"I suspect they'll bury him with full military honors, his razor, and his Brylcreem."

A car parks at the curb across the street. It's the first of the day. Through the steam above my cup, I watch a young man with acne yawn as he tugs on his uniform jacket and makes his way to the gate. He gives us a look, nods a greeting, and heads inside.

"I've been thinking about the name of your racing team," I say.

"Oh, boy."

"By your tone, I can tell you're excited by my

suggestions."

"Just no alliteration. That's all I ask."

"Agreed. I was thinking something along the lines of O'Brien Engineworks."

"Hmm." He cups his chin in his hand.

"All one word, Engineworks."

"You know, that's not half bad."

More vehicles arrive as the morning shift beckons. It's nearly eight o'clock. One by one the workers disembark, and one by one I scan their faces. Like the swirls on a fingertip, I read their lives in their expressions, all of them too young to have served in the war, all of them physically fit, most of them wishing they had a different occupation. I wonder about their names and where they'll be in twenty years.

And then I see the moon.

The bruise is shaped like a crescent. One tip touches the corner of the man's eye. It bends around his nose and ends at his upper lip, the waning residue of a hard blow to the face.

"Got you." I take my weight off the car and stare at him.

"Now what?" Derek asks, his voice low.

"Stay close."

"Copy that."

We take an angle that permits us to meet him at the gate. Even before we converge, I note the name stitched on his breast: ARLEN. It occurs to me as I smile and say good morning to him that I may be face to face with the man who killed Kaz, a man capable of violent extremes, a man who could react in unpredictable ways if accused here on the sidewalk by strangers.

"Folks," he says in way of greeting as he pushes his

way through the gate.

"May I ask you something?"

Arlen stops, turns on his heel. He wears his sandy hair in a high-top style. His eyes are gray and dim. The moon-shaped bruise on his face makes him look as if he's peering at me through a half-mask. "Yeah?"

My heartbeat feels like when you put your finger on a record and spin it faster than it's designed to move beneath the needle. "Are you Arlen Johnson?"

"Huh?" He shakes his head. "No, ma'am. Arlen Dunkirk."

"Ah, my apologies." I flash him a quick smile. "Sorry to have bothered you."

"Sure." He gives me a look and continues on his way.

The gate swings shut. A few moments later, Derek says, "And now we know his name."

"We do."

"How will we put this information to use?"

"I'll use the index when I get to work this afternoon."

"And then?"

"And then I'll find out where he lives."

Chapter Nineteen

In Which I Break and Enter

First things first. Helena has agreed to speak with
Corky in exchange for assurances that any future
testimony can be delivered in such a way that her identity
remains anonymous. She knows the names of those
shadowy figures behind the election rigging, and that
knowledge will hopefully be enough to exonerate Oliver
Bishop. When Derek and I arrive at the office, Helena's
car is already here.

Corky has brought in an extra chair and conducted a
bit of mine-sweeping so that the manly disarray has been
moved to the edges of the room. His desk is clear except
for a single folder and Betty's photograph, recently
dusted. Every window is open, but it doesn't help much.
The smell of a cigarette hangs in the air.

"Have a seat, Viv." He motions with his pen. "Ms.
Crenshaw here was just finishing up her statement."

We exchange good mornings. Helena wears a cotton
wrap dress with a tightly pleated skirt and a halter-style
top that reveals a hint of skin and serves her well in this
heat. Corky is wearing what is probably his second-best
suit, his first reserved for the courtroom. Derek has
removed his hat and balanced it on his knee, his legs
crossed. His shoes are polished in a way of which I'm
sure his Major Stanborne would approve.

"I believe that's my entire life story," Helena says. "In the proverbial nutshell."

"Okay, let me see here..." He skims his notes. "This fellow you mentioned, Pietro Modani, if he's the one responsible, I'm sure it would help Mr. Bishop's cause if I could suggest to the district attorney that there might be evidence of Modani's guilt."

"You're asking if I have any proof?"

"That would be significant, yes."

"My word isn't enough?"

Corky is about to reply, then he defers the question to me. "What do you think? How would you reply to that question? Is Ms. Crenshaw's word alone sufficient?"

Everyone looks at me. This one is easy, though. "If we were claiming that Mr. Bishop wasn't near the ballot boxes that night and that Helena were providing a physical alibi, then yes, we could build on that. But as I understand it, she has no desire at all to ever see the man again, and vice versa, given their history, in which case her word alone probably won't suffice."

Helena smiles at me. Corky nods.

"We're going to need hard evidence," I say to both of them.

"She's right." Corky drops the pen on his desk blotter and leans forward. "So, Ms. Crenshaw, what do you got for me?"

Helena takes her time. I know she's holding something back, but I don't press, mainly because I'm distracted. In my mind, Arlen Dunkirk is standing in front of Kaz and Jesse Imada and all the displaced people at the river's edge. He has a look on his face like I imagine one of the Brownshirts from Germany wore when antagonizing civilians. I'll never know exactly what was said among them that day at the warehouse. But the future flyweight champion of the world had the last word.

"Sometimes gamblers go in debt," Helena eventually says.

Corky shrugs. "Sure, happens all the time."

"I've been known to accept information as payment, in lieu of money."

"And why would you do that? You can't spend information."

"On the contrary, I've spent it very creatively in recent years. How else would an unmarried woman without a proper education keep the lights on?"

"How is this related to Mr. Bishop or Pietro Modani?"

"Pietro, I'm afraid, is a career criminal, and not a particularly talented one. He owed a certain amount to my business—which is a legitimate establishment, I might remind you."

Corky spreads his hands. "Of course."

"Pietro couldn't pay. In desperation he offered to disclose details of the council election. One of the candidates is favorable to pari-mutuel betting and the other is not, so I have an understandable interest in the results. Naturally, I accepted his terms."

"Naturally. And what is it that he told you?"

"That he'd been instructed to alter the ballot count. When it looked like he was about to be caught, he pointed the finger quite loudly at Mr. Bishop."

"A messy situation, but again, without anything hard, anything *visible*, it's just a story."

"I have the ballots."

Corky stiffens. We all do.

"Pietro Modani didn't stuff the box. He just made sure the votes for the opposition never went in."

"And you have those papers?"

She nods.

"The actual votes that were meant to be recorded by the city, those are in your possession?"

"They're not lying there on the top of my desk or hidden in my unmentionables drawer at home, but yes, I know where they are."

"And you're willing to turn them over?"

"I suppose it's possible I might be able to—"

"Wait," I say.

Everyone turns to me. Corky looks anxious. Helena looks nervous. Derek, damn him, looks amused. "I don't know this Pietro Modani from any other man on the street, but something tells me he's no mastermind. Who told him to fix the ballot box? Who gave the order?"

Corky and Derek turn to Helena, who shrugs. "I honestly don't know. You're right about Pietro. He's more weasel than wolf. Someone's behind him, and it's *that person* I don't want to cross."

"The man who does business with a shovel," I suggest, using Helena's phrase from yesterday afternoon.

She nods.

I glance at Corky. "Can we keep her safe?"

"I fought Kraut bayonets," Corky replies. "Shovels don't scare me."

I allow him all the bravado he wants; he's fearless, as far I'm concerned. "Then I believe you owe me ten dollars."

"You ever going to cut me a break, Viv?"

"Not in this lifetime."

****

That afternoon we celebrate Ms. Peele's birthday.

The cake is simple but delicious; anything made with real, non-wartime ingredients still feels like a luxury. Between calls at the switchboard, we steal bites, lick the icing from our fingers, and generally enjoy the rare and welcome distraction. Ms. Peele handles it with a diplomat's aplomb, smiling with her thin lips and gently admonishing the girls for making a fuss. And then, for just a moment, she lets us inside:

"On my eighteenth birthday, more years ago than I care to remember, a gentleman caller brought me a bouquet, but my mother refused to allow him in the house. We spent an hour exiled to the veranda, and every time I turned around, I caught her peeping at us through the drapery. I wrote in my diary that night that it was the best and worst birthday of my entire life."

We all smile, charmed by her story.

"I didn't even get a kiss on the cheek, thanks to her!"

We laugh, and for a moment she joins us. And then she makes shooing gestures and reminds us that the switchboard can't be left unattended.

An hour passes. Then two. Calls come in and cables get rerouted, an endless cycle that never seems to change, much like those pictures of a snake eating its own tail. There's a word for that image, the answer to a crossword question that I can't quite recall. Oro-something? I'm lost deeply enough in my reverie and the routine motions of my job that I don't immediately realize that Ms. Peele is standing just behind my shoulder.

"Vivian."

I spin on my stool. Have I done something wrong?

Given myself away?

"Are you well?" she asks.

"Ma'am?"

"Given your recent absences, I thought I would inquire after your health."

"I'm much better now, thank you."

"I believe you." She raises both eyebrows and gives me a rapid once-over. "In fact, I can't help but notice the change."

"The change?"

"Oh, perhaps it's nothing physical about you that's different. But if I were to put a name to it, I'd say you look...happy." She shrugs. "Or maybe not. I'm sorry for the interruption. Back to it now."

She leaves me and resumes her duties.

I smile to myself and get back to work.

****

The index has provided me with an address for Arlen Dunkirk. It's almost nine at night. Derek picked me up after my shift with his usual *Mrs. Frisco* greeting as he held open the Cord's door, and now we're parked in full shadow on a residential street on the south side of town. Neither of us has eaten supper.

"You know what they call this in the motion pictures?" he asks.

"What would that be?"

"A stakeout, if I'm not mistaken."

"That sounds awfully dramatic." I watch the house, though there's little to see. The corner lampposts found downtown have yet to be erected beyond the city's heart, but the moon is almost full tonight. The dirt driveway leading to Dunkirk's place is vacant, with no lights in the windows.

"At what point do we walk up and have a look?" Derek asks.

"How long has it been?"

"An hour, give or take."

"I don't think he's home."

"You may be right."

"Do you think it's safe?"

"Would it make any difference if it weren't?"

I turn to face him, though only his outline is visible. "What are you asking?"

"If I said it wasn't safe, would you be of a mind to go anyway?"

"Alone or escorted by a combat veteran?"

He sighs in the dark. "The latter, I suppose."

"Then yes, I'd go anyway." I open the door and climb from the car.

They built houses like this during the Depression. It's a simple rectangular clapboard structure with a steeply pitched roof and stovepipe chimney. Without a light source, I can't make out any details. A wind chime tingles from somewhere nearby.

We walk around back.

I don't know what I expect to find. In my mind, where I pace in front of a jury of Dunkirk's peers, I state the connection of which I hope to convince them: Dunkirk and his partner attempted to extort money from the Japanese refugees, but Kaz's hired muscle ran them off. In retaliation, they killed him. The murder weapon was discovered at Dunkirk's property—

Nothing has been discovered yet except an empty doghouse in the backyard. I can also make out the silhouette of a bicycle without wheels, the handle of a well pump, and the bucket below it. A single pair of trousers hangs on the line. I see no evidence of children or a wife.

The back door is not fronted by anything so homey as a porch. A stack of bricks serves as a single step. The windows remain dark. If I'm to find anything here, then I'll need to venture inside. I have nothing to show the police. Worse than this, I have nothing to show Mrs. Agawa, and it's the unfortunate kinship I feel toward her that carries me almost soundlessly to that stair made of bricks.

The door has no handle. Peering close, I can make out a simple L-shaped hook secured in an eye bolt. There is no lock, which isn't surprising. My own front door had no lock until the landlord installed one during the war, fearing that shortages might lead to looting. That never happened, at least not here.

I reach slowly for the latch.

Derek stops me by placing his fingers over mine, and for the first time since I met him one week ago, we touch.

"Are you sure this is wise?" he asks, so quietly I barely hear him.

"I don't think that matters at this point." I lift the latch, we break contact, and I let myself inside.

****

There is a kind of darkness that lures you in. We avoid the other type, turning on lights or hanging a lantern by the barn door. It impedes us, even frightens us. But certain shadows are invitations, hinting at answers not found in the light. I can sense a kitchen around me, the icebox humming, a slow drip falling from the tap.

A metallic click is followed by a flame. Derek has

produced the military man's ubiquitous Zippo lighter and now holds it before him like a tiny torch.

I give him a nod and look around.

The cramped kitchen offers little of interest, beyond a deck of cards on the table, metal dishes in the sink, and a meat grinder bolted to the countertop.

We move to the next room. It smells lived-in, a sensation I can't describe but is entirely different than the scent of vacancy. The flame reveals two thinly padded chairs, a cold hearth, and a Crosley radio in the tombstone style that was popular a decade ago but has since fallen out of fashion. The floorboards protest softly as I cross the small space. With each step, I lose faith— there is nothing to find here but the simple life of a small-time city worker. I am invading another person's space.

The invasion continues as I reach the bedroom. Derek moves directly behind me, the lighter causing the shadows to contort across the plastered walls. A crucifix hangs above the unmade bed. Occupying the nightstand are jars of pills and an overburdened ashtray.

"There's nothing here," Derek whispers.

He's right, but for some reason I don't turn and leave. Before all of this started, I joked to Corky that I experienced what the pulp magazines call extrasensory perception. I don't believe in any of that. Yet still…

I look around. There is no closet. My eyes follow the contours of those shifting shadows, trying to decipher them like an archaeologist might read ancient runes.

I kneel beside the bed.

After a moment, Derek crouches beside me.

What am I expecting to find? As I lower myself to the floor and peer under the bed, I blink a few times, my eyes continuing to adjust to the gloom. It takes me several seconds to make sense of the object hidden here, as it seems so out of context, all things considered.

"What is it?" Derek asks.

I reach below the bed and drag out a bag of golf clubs.

Derek frowns, shakes his head. In the glow of the fire, I read his expression: *It's a dead end. Put it back.*

I am inclined to agree. Arlen Dunkirk doesn't strike me as a golfer. I push the bag back—but then stop.

Derek gives me a look: *Now what?*

Just to be sure one way or the other, I slip my hand down the bag's throat. I'm reminded briefly of reaching blindly into muddy riverbank holes in search of frogs— a common pastime for bored children in the rural summer—and then my fingers close around something that doesn't belong there.

I pull out a bundle of money.

The folded bills are mostly fives and tens, perhaps two hundred dollars in all. I hold it in my hand, observing it in the meager light as if an explanation for it will suddenly appear, if I only grip it tightly enough. I'm not sure what to make of it. A person working for a sanitation crew, living in a house like this, should not have a hidden cache without some kind of remarkable explanation.

Lights flash across the window.

Derek snaps the lighter shut. *"Time to go."*

A car pulls into the dirt driveway. I ram the money back into the bag and shove the whole thing under the bed, then follow Derek from the room as quickly as I can in the dark. The car's engine shuts off when we're halfway across the living room. Derek and I are two shapes rushing through the shadows. I feel as if I'm made from air. A car door slams. We glide through the kitchen.

I open the back door as the front knob rattles somewhere behind me. I know the brick stair is below me, but I don't risk a misstep. I jump from the doorway, the breath swift in my throat. Derek eases the door closed, and then we're away. I can't recall the last time I ran anywhere. But I run now, hoping we've not been noticed, alarmed by the violent rocking of my heart, wondering as I sprint away if I've done Kaz any good at all...

Chapter Twenty

In Which I Receive Stolen Property

The night is not over yet. The Puerto Rican couple downstairs may have seen Derek stepping brisking up the stairs, but they care nothing for the world beyond their apartment. They play their records softly, given the late hour, but here in the silence of my living room, we can occasionally feel the Bomba music in the floor.

"No one drinks coffee at this time of day," I say as I pour two cups.

"It's either that or I storm your liquor cabinet."

"If only I had one." I settle into my usual chair near the telephone but don't feel at all like my usual self. When was the last time I ran like that? I dimly recall a physical education course, attended by some pre-woman version of myself.

"Are you all right?" Derek asks.

"I'm not sure that question applies anymore."

He takes a sip. "Uncle Chuck didn't mention what I'd be getting myself into when he asked me to give a gal a lift to a funeral."

"This gal is thankful."

"You're welcome. Do you think Dunkirk saw us?"

"Honestly, it was all a blur."

"And the money?"

"He's not earning it by carrying trash for the city."

"Agreed. But short of following him around all day, I don't see how we can learn anything about where he's moonlighting for extra cash."

"We don't need to follow him."

"How so?"

It's funny how one piece connects to another. Only very recently did I start to look for patterns, for relationships. Had the Agawas not given me that envelope, I suppose I would have spent the rest of my life believing that every event was separate and unrelated to the next. I tuck my legs beneath me in the chair—my shoes having been discarded moments after I entered the door—and line it all up. "Our conversation with Mr. Breckenridge led to the warehouse where the refugees are hiding. The warehouse led to the blue-and-red uniform. The blue-and-red uniform led to Arlen Dunkirk's name, and his name led to his address. His address led to the money."

"And the money leads where, exactly?"

"Not the money itself, but where it was hidden."

"A bag of golf clubs?" He lets it simmer for a moment. "So...a golf course?"

"One piece connects to another."

"Okay, say you're right. I've played at the Elm Ridge Country Club, but there must be a lot of other courses within driving distance. Seems these days you can't go five miles without seeing another one. How would we know where to start?"

I glance once at my pearl-colored telephone, then back at Derek.

He nods, spends time with his coffee. "Does this mean I may have a few rounds of golf in my immediate future?"

"How's your game?"

"Well, Sam Snead doesn't need to be looking over his shoulder, but I can hold my own with fellas from around town."

We settle the details. When it's done, I thank him again for the assistance tonight, and when he marvels aloud at the fact that I coerced him into infiltrating a man's private residence, I say coerced was not the word I'd have chosen.

He smiles and fixes his hat to his head. "Call me when you know something."

"Of course."

"Goodnight, Mrs. Frisco."

I close the door behind him and lean my back against it, exhausted but in no mood for sleep.

****

Sleep, though, must have had other ideas, because I wake up mostly dressed on top of the sheet when Satchel walks across me the next morning. It's Friday. My shift begins at one this afternoon. That leaves me—what time is it, seven?—almost six hours to discover how Arlen Dunkirk acquired all that money.

But first—the bathroom.

I turn on the radio on my way, though it's a news program and doesn't hold my attention. I pause while washing my face only when I hear a mention of the Monarchs—they're still leading the league—and then dress without giving it much thought and settle in with the telephone.

The irony of calling the switchboard for directory assistance is not lost on me. Over the next two and a half hours, here is what I learn about golf courses in the greater Kansas City area:

1. Before the war, there were at least thirty courses between here and Leavenworth on one side and Excelsior Springs on the other.

2. Thirty seems like a lot, but apparently it's true.

3. Many of those establishments have closed since hostilities started in Europe.

4. If they didn't close, they were converted to more practical purposes. The Fairfax Hills course, for example, situated between Parkwood and Klamm parks, became the foundation of new apartments for workers in the many defense plants along the river. That's where they built the B-25.

5. Of the courses remaining operational today, none provides any leads about Dunkirk.

6. Except for one. Armour Fields Golf Course has no professionals or instructors by that name who play there, but the gent who answers the phone recognizes it, just the same.

7. Arlen Dunkirk isn't a golfer. He's a caddie.

My next call routed from the switchboard is to Uncle Charlie's shop. Derek answers on the first ring.

****

Corky phones while I'm waiting on Derek to arrive. I'm finishing up a bowl of Cheerios, though I recall them being called CheeriOats not very long ago—did their name change when I wasn't looking?

In way of salutation, Corky says, "Hey, Viv, it's about those ballots."

"I'm sorry, say that again?"

"The ballots Ms. Crenshaw claims to have, can you get them?"

"I wasn't aware I'd been assigned that duty by the firm's senior partner."

"Consider me in your debt."

"Why can't you get them yourself?"

"I guess you made quite an impression on her. Says she doesn't trust anyone but you to take them off her hands, on account of some anonymous evildoer with a shovel. Look, if you need a ride over there—"

"I can manage the ride."

"So I noticed. Seems like a nice guy, by the way."

"Thanks, I think. When do you need them delivered?"

"What are you doing this morning?"

I give him an exaggerated sigh.

"Hey, as soon as you bring them, I'll clear an hour from my schedule and we can talk in detail about Kazuhiko Agawa, just like I promised. Deal?"

"You know, if you weren't Jim's best friend, you'd be completely intolerable."

"Thank God for huge favors."

****

It's eleven by the time we reach Helena's establishment. Across the street, the hand-lettered sign in front of Club Mardi Gras reminds us that JAZZ AND INTRIGUE RETURN TONIGHT AT 6:00 PM. I've never been inside.

Derek eases up to the curb and shuts off the engine. "I think I'll stay here at the car, let you take care of business inside."

I study him before replying. "You didn't shave this morning."

"I beg your pardon?"

"Sorry"—I wince and shake my head—"forgive me, I didn't mean to—"

"You're correct. I was up late with Uncle Chuck."

"It's really none of my business. I apologize. It just came out."

"You're observant. That's one reason you're good at all this."

"I don't know about that."

"It's true. At any rate, my uncle is…uh, he's sick."

"What?" I sit up a little straighter. "What do you mean?"

"The doc's not entirely sure, unfortunately. But Chuck's been having chest pains—"

"My God."

"—and though that's been going on for a few months now, we O'Briens are nothing if not stubborn fools when it comes to admitting we might need help."

"He never said anything."

"Does that surprise you?" Derek taps a finger a few times on the steering wheel. "He's the only family I have left, other than a few distant cousins I scarcely remember. That's why I spend my R&R here with him. I don't really have anywhere else to go."

"I'm sorry to hear this. Charlie's always been good to me."

"He'll be fine. He's as tough as railroad steel. Now, not to change the subject, but if you want to make it to work on time this afternoon, you better go see about acquiring those ballots."

He's right. I'll worry about Charlie later. I let myself out of the car, smooth a few wrinkles from my skirt— and then realize that Derek isn't following me. "Are you coming?"

"Like I said, I don't think so."

"Why on earth not?"

"It may be best if I stay here in the car."

"Nonsense. You're not my chauffeur, despite your jokes claiming otherwise. You're—you're my friend. So let's go before I drag you out by the arm."

He stares at me for a few moments. "So it's either accompany you or have my shoulder dislocated?"

"If you're not careful."

He smiles and climbs from the car.

****

Helena has led us to a nearly lightless brick room connected to the back of her building. The ceilings are high—at least twenty feet. The windows near the summit have no glass; leaves intrude from nearby trees. Among the bird droppings, decades of accumulated objects rest under canvas or in stacks of aging crates. Against the far wall is the fuselage from a biplane, circa 1917, long bereft of its wings.

I turn a complete circle, looking up at the spears of light that slice downward from the windows. "What is this place?"

"A time machine." Helena lights a long cigarette and watches us as we look around.

I stop near a bicycle with an enormous front wheel. Dangling from one handlebar is an open pocket watch, its hands frozen at either midnight or noon.

"Every time this property changes hands," Helena says, "the former owner bequeaths another layer of misbegotten goods to the new person. I'm told that Wild Bill Hickok's boots are buried in here somewhere."

Derek wipes a veneer of dust from the airplane, revealing the fading image of an Uncle Sam hat inside a red ring.

"It's all for sale, if you want anything," Helena tells us.

I stop near an old candlestick telephone. "I assume the ballots are here somewhere?"

"Have you located that man you're hunting?"

I look at her across the shadowy room. "I'm getting closer."

She indicates a wooden box marked LYE SOAP. "Try that one."

I approach the container, which rests upon a stack of yellowed newsprint. The lid is hinged, the boards gray with age. With one more glance at Helena, I pinch the corner of the lid with two fingers and open it. Inside is a pyramid-shaped pile of soap cakes, each one wrapped in cheesecloth. "Maybe you pointed me to the wrong hiding place."

"How old were you when Prohibition ended?"

"I'm not sure. Why? Sixteen, maybe?"

"A babe in the woods. Well, I was twenty-two, fearless and foolish in equal measures. At any rate, that crate that you're so delicately touching is an artifact from that whiskey-free day and age. If you know what I mean."

I look back at the box, the soap piled into a shape like a wedding cake. Helena was giving me the answer without quite *giving* it to me. What was it that Emily Dickinson wrote? *Tell all the truth but tell it slant.*

Asking for no further explanation, I reach down and put my fingers around the uppermost rectangle of soap.

What an odd place to find myself. Ten days ago my chief concern was learning how to properly cite my sources in a legal research paper—and now?

Tightening my grip, I lift my hand.

The entire stack of soap comes up, hollow and lightweight, a façade that isn't soap at all but a blind, underneath of which is hidden a small cigar box.

"I suppose someone used to conceal their bourbon in there," Helena says, exhaling smoke. "Now it's the resting place of the purloined letter."

I set the faux soap stack aside and remove the cigar box. It's stuffed with slips of paper allegedly removed from the ballot box by someone named Pietro Modani.

Helena extinguishes her cigarette on an antique anvil. "Remember, I never saw those before, and I want nothing more to do with your lawyer friend."

"I understand."

"I hope you do."

We say our goodbyes. She invites me to lunch tomorrow. I tell her I'm already booked for a round of Saturday golf.

Chapter Twenty-One

In Which I Recognize a Face

I have one hand on the Cord's door when the Buick
Super pulls from the opposite curb. It's a pre-war model,
black, a little worse for wear. It rolls by slowly,
intentionally. Two figures inside turn toward us, and then
the car reaches the intersection and suddenly speeds
away.

Derek looks at me over the convertible's open top.
"Friends of yours?"

I stare down the street, the car now out of sight.

He settles in behind the wheel. "Come along then.
We need to get those cigars to Mr. Schneider."

I take my seat, the wooden box in my lap. According
to the print on the lid, it supposedly holds an assortment
of Londres cigars, manufactured by R.G. Sullivan of
New Hampshire. Instead it contains the ballots intended
for a candidate who ended up losing an election for a seat
on the city council. Had these votes been counted,
perhaps that person would have won, but for the sake of
the gambling scene in Kansas City, Pietro Modani was
ordered to rig the results. Someone got suspicious and
wrongly accused Corky's client, Oliver Bishop, of
tipping the scales. And the only evidence of the crime is
right here in my hands.

It's noon by the time we reach Corky's office,

giving me an hour to wrap up my morning activities before reporting for my patriotic duty at the switchboard. Entering the building, I walk the floor where they discovered Kaz's body. There is no voice from beyond the grave that prods me as I make my way across the tiles, no ghost of Hamlet's father reminding me that a murder remains unsolved. I don't need the encouragement. I'm in this until the end, one way or the other.

****

Corky has locked the ballots in his safe. Now, minutes later, I sit with my stenographer's notebook open on my crossed legs, jotting notes while he talks:

...knew Mr. Agawa before the war...

...liked prizefighting, read the papers from front to back...

...managed to keep his job when most of the other Japs got canned or run off...

...did some cooking, too...

"I remember his corn pudding," I say with a nod.

...came to the States when he was in his twenties...

...wanted his son to be an engineer...

...learned some plumbing, helped replace a pipe under my house a few weeks back...

...his old man was a swordsmith in Osaka—

"A what?"

...the guy made swords, those curved Asian things, and was good at it...

...made 'em mainly for wealthy Jap businessmen...

...ended up dying of cancer...

...only thing Agawa had of his dad's was the last sword he forged before he died...

"Wait a minute." I hold the pen's tip against the

paper. "Kaz inherited a sword?"

"Sure, that's what he told me, anyway. Said he kept it on his mantel."

"And it was expensive?"

"I reckon so. I remember him telling me that his mother got to wear pearls on account of old rich guys wanting to be samurais or something."

"I didn't realize Japanese businessmen made it a point to carry swords."

"The swords are ceremonial. I guess having one on display in your fancy office in Tokyo makes you feel important. Who knows? But the right level of craftsmanship commands high dollar, apparently." He leans back in his chair, which creaks in protest. "Is any of this helpful?"

I softly close the notebook. I know how Mrs. Agawa got the money to pay me. At some point she sold the sword—perhaps to help cover the cost of her husband's funeral—and a portion of that sale found its way to me.

"Viv?"

"Yeah. It's helpful."

"You all right?"

"How many times have you asked me that since you came back from France?"

After a moment, he gives me a smile of rare gentleness. "I'm sorry. I won't ask again."

"Thanks. Because the answer's always the same."

Before I leave for work, Corky extends Betty's invitation to a Saturday evening dinner party. He waves off my initial shake of the head and says that Gene and Darby will also be in attendance, so come on, Viv, it won't be the same without you, and on and on until I acquiesce. Derek accepts the offer to join us, which makes it six for dinner at the Schneider house tomorrow night, unless I am lucky and get hit by a bus beforehand.

Derek says surely it can't be that bad.

I hope he's right. I spend the next eight hours living by rote, conducting the drab business of my job life while my real life—in which I masquerade as a Pinkerton detective—waits for the morning so I can track down a caddie with secrets to hide.

****

Armour Fields Golf Course stretches between State Line Road and Ward Parkway, a lovely landscape of low hills and satisfying fairways. The Saturday morning sun reflects from the Cord's chrome as we get out and observe the vaguely colonial structure that serves as the clubhouse.

Here is what I know about golf, little enough to be compacted into a haiku:

Morning on the green:
people slashing at the grass,
trying to score low.

"What if Arlen Dunkirk isn't here today?" Derek asks. "Just because he's a caddie doesn't mean—"

"Actually, it *does* mean."

"Come again?"

"Given the game's popularity, every would-be professional is at their home course whenever it's open for business. Amateurs tote their own gear, but anyone with aspirations wouldn't be caught without a caddie. If Dunkirk is making the kind of money worth hiding under his bed, then he won't miss a chance to keep that going."

"Well, by now I've come to trust your instincts. Besides, I'll never pass up an opportunity to play." He retrieves his clubs from the trunk, and then we make our way up the pebbled walk.

I am wearing the closest thing I own to an actual golfing dress, white with short sleeves and blue leather buttons all the way down the front. Derek, however, appears to be clipped from the sports pages, authentic, athletic, dapper beyond reason. He even has these special gloves.

"Is something the matter?" he asks.

"You look the part, I'll give you that."

"Thanks. Maybe one day I'll have a mortgage to worry about, but until then I suppose I fritter away my salary on striped socks that I wear for only one occasion."

We step through the clubhouse doors. The interior is airy and decorated mainly in white, with paintings of famous golfers—the ones you hear about on the radio. But if not for the brass placards beneath each one, I wouldn't know Byron Nelson from Bobby Jones.

The clerk is a young man who is likely a university student, pumped full of weekend enthusiasm. He slides an open log book to Derek as he accepts the green fee from me, chatting all the while about the amenities offered here at Armour Fields. I skim the few names that have arrived here before us this morning—there aren't many, as it's only half past eight—but see no mention of Dunkirk.

At this point Derek and the clerk indicate that I'll need to rent some clubs.

"Can't I use yours?"

"I'm six feet two. How tall are you?"

"All right, I see your point. I suppose I assumed that a nine iron was universal."

We take care of the arrangements, and soon I am

suitably equipped. Derek picks up his clubs and motions toward the French doors that lead to the first tee. "Shall we?"

"How much do you charge for lessons?"

"How much is it worth to you?"

"Is there a discount if I'm actually here with ulterior motives?"

"You do realize, yes, that complete concentration is necessary to a good game."

"You make it sound so serious."

He holds open the door for me. "Something tells me this is going to be an interesting morning."

"Let's hope so." I step out into the sun.

****

"And...that's what we call a slice," Derek says, watching my ball fly toward the sycamores on the right.

"This is harder than it looks."

"You'll get a handle on it soon." He bends down and places his ball on the tee. This is our second hole. Derek is somehow already one under par.

I see the appeal of this kind of Saturday. Mine are often spent with a book. And there's always the wash in need of doing. But this is different: sharper, clearer, a thing not just to do but to enjoy. Against the dazzling green of the grass and trees are the multicolored outfits of the golfers themselves, summertime heroes and heroines with the war behind them and nothing but easy eight-foot putts in front.

Derek blasts the ball from the tee. I lose sight of it in the sky, relocate it, and watch it land a triumphant distance away.

"I once played a game at night," he tells me as we walk in the direction my ball disappeared.

"I wasn't aware that one could golf in the dark."

"Not well, true enough. But it was a full moon that night, so that helped."

"I assume this was a caper among Air Corps friends?"

"You are very intuitive, Mrs. Frisco."

"What about a woman?"

"I'm sorry?"

"Have you ever golfed with a woman before?"

"Certainly. That's one of the reasons for the sport's popularity. Everyone can play."

"Some better than others." I spot my ball, an Easter egg half-hidden in the tall grass. "Do I have to attempt to hit it from here?"

Derek retrieves my ball from the rough and tosses it to the middle of the fairway. "We call that a mulligan."

"Is that legal?"

"Strictly speaking?"

"Right. I won't tell if you won't tell." We walk and talk, my mulligans multiply, and at some point I realize that two hours have passed with my mind occupied by nothing but conversation. I'm perspiring lightly into my dress as the day warms, and Derek's suggestion of a clubhouse visit is perfectly timed. I drink an iced lemonade. I refresh myself in the ladies' room. And when I emerge, Derek is gazing from the big plate-glass window, his back facing me, his hat in his hands.

I study him. I write his story in my mind.

Once upon a time there lived a boy who dreamed of the sky. He built planes from balsa wood and jumped from trees, hoping this would be the time his arms caught the air. As he grew up, so did his aspirations. He lost his family through the years, save for one stubborn uncle, and joined a flying squadron the moment he was given the chance. He fought a terrible enemy and prevailed. Upon returning home, he taught his craft to others but missed the action. One day he struck a pose in front of a window, causing his biography to be composed without him even knowing it.

I approach and stand beside him. "How's the view?"

"Getting better by the moment."

I keep my eyes straight ahead, suddenly uncertain of everything. The scene outside is too ordinary for what's within. Perhaps foolishly, I open my mouth, wondering what will come out, but then Derek says, "Well, I'll be damned."

I glance up at him, then follow his gaze.

Arlen Dunkirk has entered the clubhouse lobby, and I recognize his companion instantly. Dunkirk carries a set of clubs. He wears khaki trousers and a short-sleeved white shirt. The bruise on his face has faded almost entirely.

Beside him, chatting it up with the clubhouse clerk, is Wallace Breckenridge.

I turn back around before the Nazi-hunter and sword-collector sees me. The last time we met, he served us iced tea and regaled us with stories of the urban battles in Aachen. Breckenridge owns the warehouse where Dunkirk took a punch from Automatic Mahone.

Derek has also swiveled back to the window. Without looking at me, he says, "I suppose we'd call this an interesting development."

"What do we do now?"

"I think I'm the one who should be asking that question."

"Let's just wait."

"Roger."

Breckenridge makes a comment about cigars on the ninth hole, laughs at his own joke, then two sets of footsteps move behind us. The French doors open, then close.

I silently count to five, then relax my stance.

"What now?" Derek asks.

"I'll resist the urge to go chasing after him."

"Right. The idea of stalking him across the course seems a little preposterous."

I approach the doors and move aside a curtain embroidered with little golf flags. Breckenridge and Dunkirk stroll beneath the sun toward the first tee. "We'll give them a little room, let them play ahead for a while."

"Got it. Followed by what?"

"We'll pick up the pace, and at some point we'll intentionally bump into him."

"And then what?"

"I don't know yet." I pick up my rented clubs from where I left them beside the door. "But I'm sure I'll think of something."

Chapter Twenty-Two

In Which I Confront the Suspect

The sixth hole is the trickiest. It's an expansive par five with a fish pond on the left. Only the Greek heroes on the course try to sail one over the pond, smashing the ball like Achilles, while the more earthbound among us settle for going around. The hole is also on a visible incline, foiling the approach shot of many an eager golfer. That's where I make my calculated encounter with Mr. Breckenridge, a few moments after he misjudges the slope.

"So very close!" I say from behind him as his ball veers away from the hole.

He offers a little wave of acknowledgement without really seeing us, the half-scowl on his face revealing his opinion of *so very close*. Putter still in hand, he marches toward his ball, Dunkirk at his heels.

"I believe we've met, Mr. Breckenridge."

That stops him. He turns and faces us as we advance. He's wearing an Englishman's sporting attire, complete with a pleated belt and matching hat. He looks like a man about to embark on a fox hunt. One week has passed since we visited him. Apparently he's not forgotten my name. "Mrs. Frisco, isn't it?"

"It is. And this is—"

"Mr. O'Brien, of course." His scowl replaced by an

amicable smile, Breckenridge extends a gloved hand to Derek, and then to me, and over his shoulder Arlen Dunkirk is giving me the eye. "Had no idea the two of you played. You should have mentioned that. Could've gotten you a discount on your green fees."

"A kind gesture," I reply. "To be honest, this is my first time."

"Rookie, eh? And what do you think of it so far?"

"The view from the rough isn't as bad as they imply."

He laughs. "What about you, O'Brien? First-timer or an old salt?"

"Somewhere in the middle, most likely." Derek indicates Breckenridge's ball. "I wouldn't want to interrupt your putt."

"Ah, that was already spoiled, I'm afraid. These damnable hills have always gotten the better of me. But I suppose that's why I keep coming back. One day I'll turn the tables. Mind if I knock it in?"

"By all means."

Breckenridge gives his putter a spin and then settles in over the ball. A predefined peace descends that happens only at this moment, for this specific activity. I glance at Dunkirk, but his full attention is on the ball.

Corky Schneider once told me a story of the war. After eliminating an enemy pillbox, Corky and his mates discovered a makeshift putting green behind the embankment. Apparently the Germans spent their downtime like any other young men anywhere in the world, playing games and gazing at manhandled photographs of Lana Turner.

Breckenridge taps the ball, which makes a perfect line and drops into the hole.

"Good shot, boss," Dunkirk says.

"Thanks, but it's one good shot too many." He marks his score on a pad.

As Derek heads toward his own ball, which stopped about twenty feet downslope from the hole, I walk to Breckenridge as he's stowing his pad in a shirt pocket. "Do you mind if I ask you a question?"

"My advice is don't take up this hobby unless you're fond of disappointment."

"I'll keep that in mind. But it's about our visit last week."

"Yes, after you informed me of that man's death, I had my secretary send a note of condolence to his family. I was very sorry to hear what happened."

"I'm sure Mrs. Agawa appreciated that." It is at this point, seconds before I ask if he was aware that refugees had been sheltering in his warehouse, that I realize the danger: Breckenridge's caddie might have murdered Kaz, and he's standing within arm's reach.

"Your question, Mrs. Frisco?"

"Right. It's just…" I improvise and turn to Dunkirk. "I believe you and I have a friend in common."

Dunkirk looks surprised at having been addressed. A lock of hair hangs between his eyes. He blinks a few times as if trying to make sense of my statement, then frowns. "Come again, ma'am?"

"I'm wondering if you know Jesse Imada."

"Jesse who?"

"Imada. He's an editor, or at least he was until he was fired because he's Japanese."

"Ma'am, I have no idea—"

"You probably didn't bother to ask his name." An unusual warmth rises in my chest. It's been a while since

I was really angry—years, actually—but whether this man is a killer or not, he's at least a bully who tried to shake down a bunch of refugees for no other reason than he thought he could get away with it. Confronting him is likely a bad idea, but the words come out of me as if they understand my need to let them go. "Too bad for you that Kazuhiko Agawa showed up, and he brought a friend."

Breckenridge stares at me. Twenty feet away, Derek is frozen over his ball, watching us.

"Any of that ring a bell?" I ask.

After a while, Dunkirk shifts the weight of the golf bag on his shoulder, wipes the band of summer sweat from his forehead, and says, "I think you got the wrong guy."

"Have I?

"Yes, ma'am."

We look at each other like that for longer than is comfortable for anyone here. I don't know what will happen next, and in this instant I don't care. I don't have Kelly Mahone's jab, but if I did...

Breckenridge clear his throat. "It seems we may have a bit of miscommunication going on, wouldn't you say?" He intervenes and breaks the spell, dispatching Dunkirk to the next tee with a toss of his hand. To me, he says, "Care to tell me what this is all about, Mrs. Frisco?"

"I'm investigating a crime."

"You told me you were friends of the dead man's family."

"It's more than that now."

"So I see. You believe that Mr. Dunkirk is caught up in all of that?"

"He was slugged in the face for harassing innocent

people."

"Is that a fact?"

"Yes, sir."

"And what were the circumstances of this altercation?"

"Maybe you should ask him."

"How about I ask you?"

Derek approaches but says nothing, putter over his shoulder.

"Arlen Dunkirk had a motive for wanting to hurt Mr. Agawa."

"Mr. Agawa was Japanese," Breckenridge reminds me. "The entire country has a motive."

"You're blaming a Kansas City custodian for a military attack in Hawaii that happened five years ago?"

Breckenridge gives me a patronizing sigh and shakes his head. "Mrs. Frisco, unless you have some particular—"

"Evidence?"

"Yes, actually."

"The *altercation* happened at one of your properties, just like the murder."

Either Wallace Breckenridge is a fair actor or this information surprises him. I'm not sure either way, but he narrows his eyes. "Please explain."

I tell him what I know—most of it, at least. I assure him that the refugees are using his warehouse only as a waystation and have no intention of residing there permanently. All the while I study his face. This is a man who has engaged in urban tank warfare. I find no ready answers there.

"These families are there right now?" he asks.

"Yes."

"And I'm supposed to approve of their trespassing?"

"They won't be there for much longer."

"I hope you're right. You believe that Arlen is connected to the murder?"

"I'm just following leads, sir."

"He's a little hotheaded, sure, but if you're suggesting he might have killed a man out of revenge for a bruised nose, I'm not certain I agree." He looks at Derek. "What about you?"

"Oh, I don't know, I'm really just here as the hired help. But I've learned to trust Mrs. Frisco's instincts."

"Do those instincts say I should confront my caddie, ask him where he was on the night of the killing, or some such thing? Is that what you two are proposing?"

Derek leans on his putter like a cane. "An innocent man was beaten to death, Mr. Breckenridge, in a building that you own. If I were you, that would pique my curiosity. I'd want answers."

"And what do the police think about all this?"

Before Derek has a chance to reply, I say, "He's a Jap and nobody cares. Except me." I heave my bag of clubs and head to the next hole, par four, where Dunkirk is waiting.

****

I have never seen violence in real life, right in front of me. The newsreels are as close as I ever came to the war, and Kaz's serene body as close as I ever came to the aftermath of murder. The boxing matches one week ago were as intense as anything I've ever witnessed in person.

Arlen Dunkirk could change all of that. He watches me all the way to the tee. Too young to have served but too old to be called a boy, he is that unfortunate age that can lay claim neither to liberating Europe nor to losing a father overseas. Those honors denied him, perhaps he has taken to harassing political refugees as a kind of substitute strength.

"Why are you here?" he asks as soon as I'm close enough to hear him.

I keep walking, my heartbeat accelerating with every step. Surely he won't try anything in such a public place. The July sun forces him to squint. Protected somewhat by my hat, I take advantage of the light and position myself so he's looking directly into it. "Would you mind if I ask you a few questions?"

"Seems like I may not have a choice."

"Did you know Mr. Imada?"

"Yeah, I guess we met. They all look the same to me, really."

"Was there a fight in the warehouse?"

"They got no right to be there."

"Perhaps not. Did you demand money?"

"Like I said, they got no right. Maybe I was doing them a favor by not telling Mr. Breckenridge they were camped out where they shouldn't be."

"And you wanted money for this favor?"

"Guy's gotta make a living. Look, lady—"

"Mrs. Frisco."

"—whoever you are, no cop in this city cares if somebody gives a bunch of Japs a hard time for squatting on someone else's property."

"You're right, unfortunately."

"Then pardon me, but what the hell are we doing here?"

"One of those men was beaten to death."

Dunkirk opens his mouth, ready to tell me off, but

then he bites his lip and says nothing. To his credit, he appears taken aback by this news.

"Kazuhiko Agawa was murdered."

"I don't know anything about that."

"He was the man who was accompanied by the boxer. You remember *him*, don't you?"

He nods.

"What happened after he punched you, Mr. Dunkirk?"

"I bled all over the floor, thank you very much."

"And later?"

"And later what?"

"When did you next see Mr. Agawa?"

"Never. Haven't seen him since. And I damn sure didn't kill him or anyone else."

"Then who did?"

"How the fu—" He smiles without humor, a dark crescent across his face. His gray eyes are watery pale in the sunlight. "I don't know anything about that. I haven't been out to the river since. Haven't spoken to a single Jap. Hell, haven't even *seen* one. If you think I had something to do with a guy getting himself whacked, then you're way off track."

Is he lying? I've heard that Hoover's men in Washington have a machine that can tell if a person is telling the truth. All I have is the slant of the sun in his face and my own intuition, neither of which is a trustworthy tool.

"Can I go now? I'm getting paid to tote clubs today, and like everybody else, I need the money, if you don't mind."

Maybe J. Edgar would have slapped Dunkirk across the face, just on general principles. As for me, I simply turn and walk away, far less certain of myself than when I arrived.

Chapter Twenty-Three

In Which I Am Infiltrated

I have never been to war, but I have used a mimeograph machine.

The cantankerous device accepts page one of my paper titled "Implications of the Public Safety Act of 1939: Regulation and Taxation." I crank the handle, the big drum spins, and a copy of the page rolls into the basket. The ink is somewhat purple and smells faintly of blueberries. The second copy gets stuck to the roller, of course, and on the next attempt the page prints unevenly, but half an hour later I have three acceptable copies of my assignment, and the battle concludes with me more or less the victor.

Derek and I are in the library at 9th and Locust on Saturday afternoon, a few hours removed from the golf course. I find him browsing the collection of paintings and early photographs from the American West.

"A fan of cowboys?" I ask, taking up a place beside him.

"Isn't every boy?"

"Stagecoaches and trail songs aren't things you outgrow?"

"Well, I'm not a young lad anymore, but just the same, I always turn on the radio when it's time for *The Lone Ranger*."

"Can't blame you for that. Are you ready to go?"

"Got what you needed?"

I look down at the papers in my hands, but I'm not thinking about school and Monday morning deadlines. If Arlen Dunkirk was telling the truth, then I'm destined to disappoint the Agawa family with my next telephone call.

Derek reads my thoughts. "Back to square one?"

"Seems that way."

"You're sure he wasn't lying to you?"

"I'm not sure of anything at this point. Come on." We make our way to the car.

Once we're inside, Derek checks his watch. "Do we have time to change before the Schneider dinner?"

"I was hoping you'd forget."

"Oh, it won't be that bad. If nothing else, it'll take your mind off all this grim business for a while." He fires up the Cord and lets the engine idle. "What do you say?"

He's probably right. My Saturday nights are usually spent alone.

"Well?"

I relent with a sigh. "Hi-yo, Silver, I suppose."

He smiles and throws the car into gear.

****

A Saturday evening social in the dining room of Corky and Betty Schneider looks remarkably like a Norman Rockwell painting. Corky invited us yesterday, so here we are, Derek across from me in a three-button, notched-lapel sport coat in camel tan, with dark trousers, the bourbon in his glass even darker. On one side of the dining table is the lord of the manor, his wife on the opposite end in a dress I've never seen before. Its deep blue color makes Betty's black hair even blacker. She is as radiant as a store-window ad. Also in attendance are Gene and Darby Skinner, neither of whom I've seen since the barbecue on the Fourth. Gene, in his usual meandering manner, is talking about bees.

"...I've nothing against a good jar of honey, mind you, but having a beekeeper move in next door, hives and all, is a little disconcerting."

"Are they aggressive, these bees?" Derek asks him.

"The neighbor tells me I've nothing to fear unless I go poking them with a rake." Gene's face is narrow, the hair at his temples beginning to gray. He served stateside in the war, using his editorial background to produce press releases for the army. His most peculiar trait is his habit of running up and down the streets every morning for exercise. "But still, every time I get close to the fence, I can hear them over there, churning up a storm."

"Stay away from the fence then," Corky suggests.

Darby shakes her head. "Then how would he ever eavesdrop on our neighbors?"

"Does he do that a lot?"

"Are you kidding? He uses a U-boat periscope to peer into their backyard."

Everyone chuckles, even Gene. Darb has always been funny, and I envy her for it.

From there, the dinner guests converse in a kind of practiced ricochet, phrases and gestures bouncing off one another in a lively manner. We each have our role:

Corky Schneider, as the magnanimous host.

Betty Schneider, as the flirtatious housewife.

Gene Skinner, as the rambling philosopher.

Darby Skinner, as the comic relief.

Derek O'Brien, as the suave outsider.

And in a small supporting role, me, as the girl

detective.

Our little play continues into its second act, our dinner eaten, the cigarettes out, and while talk moves to this year's election for Kansas governor, I'm thinking not about periscopes or politics but about brooms.

Kaz was cleaning the lobby when he was murdered. Corky showed up around eight in the morning and discovered the body. Kaz had arrived early and let himself in with what I assume to be a maintenance key. No one else was in the building, though the streets outside were already busy with traffic. He was sweeping the floor when he died, struck on the head with some kind of bludgeon that no one would ever find because it had probably been thrown in the Missouri River by now. The police had decided he was killed by a passing racist who was taking out his leftover wartime frustrations on a random Japanese victim. If so, the killer had been downtown at seven-something in the morning, had spotted Kaz entering the building and taking up his broom, and had followed him inside on a homicidal whim.

I do not believe it happened that way.

"…but I for one could use some fresh air," Corky is saying. "What do you say we take this out on the porch?"

"Sounds classier to call it a veranda," Darby suggests.

"Veranda it is."

We all stand, smoothing out our laps and dropping our napkins on the table. Derek is charming them all to tiny pieces with his easy manner, and Darby gives me a wink, but I pretend not to understand her coded message.

"We have dessert in the icebox," Betty says. "I'll bring some for everyone, whether you're still hungry or not."

"I'll give you a hand," Gene offers, "assuming I can sample whatever it is before we feed it to the rest of these heathens."

While Betty and Gene head to the kitchen, the rest of us take up wicker chairs overlooking the lawn and the croquet balls, Derek and Corky deep in a sudden discussion of motor oil brands—of all ridiculous things. Beside me, Darby tells the story of the time when Gene dragged her up to Wisconsin to try fly fishing and he ended up in the hospital to have a hook removed from his knee.

My second failed theory is this: the killer was already in the building when Kaz arrived for work that day, and the murder was the result of an interrupted robbery. Except there were no signs of a break-in and nothing was stolen. When I eliminate the other possibilities as unrealistic, I am left with the certainty that Kaz's death was premeditated. He was trailed into the building by someone who knew him and harbored a particular reason to want him dead.

"Are those new shoes?" Darby asks me.

My legs are crossed. I give my dangling foot a shake. "I've been splurging recently."

"Splurging becomes you. By all means, keep it up."

Kaz was one of the top ten meekest men in America, so I scratch the first item from a quick list of why someone wanted to kill him:

1. He angered someone.
2. He knew too much.
3. He owed money.

Assuming he hadn't led a double life and moonlighted as a criminal, Kaz was murdered for one of those two remaining reasons. And if his family had been able to produce over nine hundred dollars to employ me, he probably could've held off a loan shark for a while longer. Which leaves only a single motive remaining.

Corky lifts his voice in the direction of the kitchen and calls, "Hey, didn't someone near and dear to my heart mention a dessert?"

"Your wish is my command, darling." Betty and Gene appear with a serving tray and six little saucers of raspberry tarts, topped with quickly melting whipped cream. I accept with a smile, the conversation turns to the rising local property taxes, and silently I ask myself a question that, for now, has no answer.

What did Kazuhiko know that got him killed?

****

Night has fallen by the time Derek drops me off. I watch the Cord's taillights fade, and then I remove my hat and wipe a crease of sweat from my forehead as I make my way to the stairs. As far as dinner parties are concerned, I rate this one a bit higher than usual, most likely because I didn't go alone. Usually I'm the odd number in the group—the three or the five—so it was nice to be part of an even number this time.

I'm putting my foot on the first step to my apartment when a voice rises from the darkness behind me:

"You had visitors tonight, Mrs. Frisco."

Startled, I turn quickly. Nat Looper stands in the darkness, a bottle in his hands.

I let out the breath I was holding. "You frightened me."

"Apologies, madam."

"What visitors?"

"Men in suits."

"What men?"

"Couldn't say."

"They came to my apartment?"

"More than that."

"What do you mean?"

"They let themselves inside."

"They went into my home?"

"Yes, ma'am."

I look up the stairs, not knowing what to expect.

"They left a long time ago."

"Did you see their faces?"

"Not really."

"How about their car?"

"Sure. Dark. Big."

Something occurs to me. "A black Buick Super?"

"Could've been. Yes, ma'am."

"And you're certain they're gone?" Yesterday morning, two men in a car like that watched me emerge from a meeting with Helena Crenshaw, the stolen ballots stuffed in my purse. "You saw them leave?"

"You be careful, Mrs. Frisco." He ambles off into the night.

I rush up the stairs.

The door bears no evidence of what the police call forced entry. The landlord only recently installed a lock. I can't remember if I turned the bolt or not when I left. Inside, I throw on all the lights. Everything appears as I left it…or does it?

Satchel twirls between my ankles. I ignore him. When you live alone, no one else is around to move things once they're in place. The afghan you keep folded twice near the worn reading chair for colder nights is never taken up and used by someone else who folds it differently when they're done. Things like that. I move slowly, breathing lightly, sensing more than seeing the subtle disturbances. The books on the shelf are still neat, but no longer are they aligned precisely the same way. I know for a fact that *The Heart is a Lonely Hunter* was positioned to the left of *A Tree Grows in Brooklyn* because they are usually shelved by the year I read them, but now these two are reversed.

I take down Margaret Mitchell, fearful I've been robbed, but the money remains inside.

For the next several minutes, I inspect the rooms of my small apartment, picking up speed as I go. At last I feed the cat. While he eats at my feet, I put my hands on my hips and accept the fact that my invaders didn't find what they were seeking because the stolen election ballots are locked in Corky's safe. That's the good news.

The bad: Someone knows I have proof of an election crime, and they're stalking me.

Chapter Twenty-Four

In Which I Arm Myself

On Sunday morning, I watch a pot and wait for it to boil. Actually it's a kettle, my coffee grounds on standby. I slept poorly last night, imagining a hand on my apartment doorknob or a dark car parked just below my window. I telephoned Derek as soon as the hour was decent. When he heard about my unknown visitors, he swore, apologized for it, then said he was on his way.

On the stovetop, very little is happening.

The fastest runner I ever knew was the Burkes boy who lived on the edge of town when I was in the ninth grade. I once saw him outrun several upperclassmen who were intent on doing whatever older boys did to younger ones as part of the ritual of growing up. They never caught him. This memory returns to me now as I stand in front of the stove because our teacher once said that Burkes was faster than bubbles in a boiling pot. That's always stuck with me, though I don't know why.

****

"And you're sure nothing was stolen?" Derek asks.

We sit at my kitchen table, the windows open, the sounds of church bells barely heard in the distance. "I don't have much to steal, but everything's here."

"You're certain this is related to the Oliver Bishop case?"

194

"Helena was hiding ballots that might have changed the outcome of the election. Someone found out that she had them, and they were staking her out the day you and I paid her a visit."

"Why would they assume you're involved?"

"I suppose they don't know for sure, but I associate with a lawyer who used to be a private investigator. And I've been asking a lot of questions around town recently. If I were them, I'd be suspicious of me, too."

"All right. But who is *them*?"

"I wish I knew. They work for the man with the shovel."

Derek doesn't look happy. He broods over his coffee.

We share thoughts without speaking them. Sundays are not made for this kind of conversation.

After a while, Derek says, "The fellow who gave those ballots to Ms. Crenshaw—"

"Pietro Modani."

"Right. Modani. She referred to him as a career criminal. There's no telling what manner of illegal schemes Modani's involved with, which means we have no idea what to expect from those two men in the black car. They could be totally harmless, or they could be—" He moves his hand in a way that says they could be anything, including the kind of people who sink bodies in cement.

"What do you suggest?"

"I'm not certain this is safe anymore."

"You may be right."

"Time to call it quits?"

"That's not what I was thinking."

"I assumed as much. What, then? If strangers are

entering your home uninvited, there's no way to predict what they might do next. Do you own a firearm?"

It's odd that his question doesn't surprise or alarm me. That's how rapidly my sedentary life has transformed. I shake my head. "No. But I know where to get one."

****

I lost track of how many bullets I made during the war. I used to count them, when I first started, numbering them by box of fifty or crate of five hundred. Like everyone else, I knew the conflict would end by Christmas, but when enough Christmases had passed, I gave up both counting and a certain degree of hope.

In addition to producing the B-25 medium bomber over at Fairfax, my hometown produced general-purpose ammunition for everything from small sidearms to vehicle-mounted machine guns. Taking up half a city block on Franklin Avenue, where the river aims north, the former steel plant was open sixteen hours a day, six days a week, but now the entire area has been abandoned. The factory closed last year when the war officially ended, though much of the machinery remains inside, awaiting sale by the government. The place has been deserted for nine months, and as today is Sunday, the nearby streets see little traffic. We are alone and unobserved as we climb from the car and make our way to the sagging fence.

"I thought you said this used to be a munitions factory," Derek says. "All the bullets in the world won't help us without a gun to fire them."

"We didn't make guns, but we tested the ammunition. A quality control clerk took random samples off the line. We had to keep guns of all calibers on hand."

"That must have been an impressive collection."

"Not really. Most of the weapons were outdated or otherwise decommissioned. Some were captured from the enemy. A few were from the previous war. It wasn't anything that could've been used reliably on the front lines."

"And the federal government just left a bunch of these old test guns lying around?"

"Everything was locked up when not in use."

"They let you keep your keys when they shut down?"

"The steel storage cabinets are held shut with combination locks."

"Ah. And you still remember the proper combination."

"I guess we'll see. There might not be anything left."

The gates have fallen into disrepair. The metal signs warn us to keep away or face prosecution, but they hang at awkward angles because one of the supporting posts leans only a few degrees away from falling completely. The two gates meet unevenly, leaving a gap in between.

For the first time since I met him ten days ago, Derek looks nervous.

"What's the matter?"

"You know if we get caught doing this…"

"No one is anywhere nearby. Look around. This place has been vacant for months."

"I hear you. But still…"

"If we have to explain ourselves, I'll just say I was showing an Army Air Corps officer the place where I used to make bullets for his Mustang."

He considers this and nods. "Not bad, as far as cover

stories go."

I understand his hesitation but feel detached from it. Every passing day, those things that used to concern me lose a bit of their urgency. I entered and searched Arlen Dunkirk's home illegally, and then someone did the same to me. And they might not be finished with me yet. So here we are.

I turn sideways and slip through the gap.

A carpet of weeds covers the parking lot of compacted dirt. Derek and I approach the nearest of the building's many doors. Much of the flotsam of my former occupation remains: the signs about worker safety, the warnings of possible spies on the assembly line, the endless cigarette butts. On summer days, when the air inside was unbearable, we ate our lunches from metal pails while seated on these same railroad timbers. Our shift manager would point the radio at the open window so we could listen to the news of Belgian villages, delivered by broadcasters with a transatlantic accent.

Derek and I say nothing, absurdly afraid our whispered voices might carry a quarter-mile to the nearest intersection and give us away. I lead him around to the bay doors on the east side, one of which never quite seated perfectly in its locking grooves on the ground. The same old concrete blocks are still stacked here. I remember the day they were delivered, intended to become walls for an additional restroom in the event the factory needed to hire black people in order to increase output. The new toilet was never built, and the bricks remain.

I bend down and give the latch a practiced shake. It comes loose on the second try, and with Derek's assistance, I haul open the big door.

The space within the ammunition factory is dusty and mostly dark. Long tables built of cylindrical runners take up much of the floor space. The presses remain: hand-presses mounted to steel tabletops and floor presses designed for the larger calibers. The hoppers for the gunpowder are no longer here, probably auctioned off to private industry. But nearly everything else remains, trapped in time. Empty brass cartridges, scattered everywhere, form messy constellations from one end of the building to the other.

Derek turns on his flashlight.

The beam is weak and does little to part the shadows. Less than a year ago, wearing my unbecoming overalls and carrying a tray of primers, I walked across this floor with Matilda Seavers.

"I'm telling you, being a mother isn't always as rewarding as it's supposed to be," Matilda says, a blond curl hanging between her eyes. *"I have my soaking moments, you know."*

I give her a glance. "Soaking moments?"

"In the bathtub, yes. You soak and soak and wonder if you're as happy as you planned to be, back when you were a girl and it all seemed so far away, and before you know it, the bath water is cold."

"I'll take your word for it."

"Are you sorry you and Jim—you know."

"Never had children? No." I put the requisite smile on my face. "They say everything happens for a reason, right?"

"Is that what they say? Sometimes I wonder..."

I give a little start when Derek touches my arm. "Are you all right?"

"I'm not sure."

"Do you want to leave?"

"Not yet. It's this way." I lead him beyond the rows of wooden worktables, scattering a few sparrows that have gained access through fissures in the roof. I could probably find my way even without the flashlight's help, as I spent most of the war here. Matilda rarely worked a double shift because of her kids. Me, I had only a cat, and Satchel always forgave me with only minimal complaint.

The north wall is comprised of a series of cages, inside of which we used to store the gunpowder and the test weapons. A combination lock is embedded within each door. When the plant first opened, each door had a different combination, for security's sake, but everyone quickly decided that convenience was more important. On most days, every door was propped open with a scrap of wood or a bag of sheet-metal screws, in violation of various regulations, but no one ever cared.

Today those cages are closed. When released, the doors are pulled shut by springs, the bolts snapping into place. I approach the next-to-last on my right, peering through the thick grating while Derek shines his light inside.

"Is this the one?" he asks.

"We'll see." I put my hand on the dial, close my eyes, and remember.

"What do German pilots eat for breakfast?" Matilda asks.

"I don't know. What?"

"Luftwaffles."

I smile and turn the dial. After the third rotation, I move the L-shaped handle downward, and the bolt slides back.

"Well done," Derek whispers.

Inside the cage are several wooden crates, toolboxes, and dented buckets. They're filled with broken guns. Most of the weapons are missing various pieces of themselves, mainly grips, sights, or safetys. Stocks are cracked and hammers bent. Many probably still fire, but some certainly do not. Most of the better ones were already carted off.

We dig through the piles. With only one flashlight between us, the process is slow. We ignore the rifles as impractical and concentrate on the handguns. Derek takes his time inspecting each one. I am less studious, ready to be away from this place. I should probably return to the river warehouse and let Jesse Imada know that he might have visitors. Who knows if Breckenridge will allow the families to remain there? Maybe I should have found some way of telling Breckenridge what happened without revealing where it occurred. Have I put the refugees in danger?

And then I find it.

The small black semi-automatic looks to be in decent repair. From the size of it, I'm guessing it's chambered in .32 caliber. The writing embossed on the side of the slide is in German. I hand it to Derek.

He examines it in the flashlight beam. "It's a Sauer."

"Is that all right?"

"You want us to carry a Nazi pistol?"

"You know that line about the beggars and choosers?"

He ejects and inspects the magazine. He uses his thumb to push out eight bullets, then returns them. "It needs a little oil, but I suppose it's the best we can do."

He holds it out to me.

I gently push it back. "Can you keep it for now?"

He nods, then slips the gun into his trouser pocket. "Shall we adjourn?"

As I hurry us across the factory floor toward the daylight of the doorway, I wonder what Matilda Seavers is doing these days. I've not seen her since the last hour of the war. Wherever she is, I hope she's surrounded by her children and never has to make another bullet again.

Chapter Twenty-Five

In Which I Take the Blame

As the Cord stops at an intersection while a family crosses the street to the Holy Trinity Orthodox Church, I try to recall what I was doing the Sunday morning before all of this began. Most likely I was sleeping late, reading a few chapters in whatever novel women like me were supposed to read, and tidying the house in preparation for a new and repetitive week.

Item of contrast: this morning. I have snuck onto *verboten* government property and stolen a Reich-made handgun. Give me a few hours and I'll probably be tying damsels to railroad tracks and smoking Venezuelan cigars.

"Something amusing?" Derek asks. He must have caught me smiling.

"Where would you be on a Sunday morning if you weren't here?"

"Where would I be or where would I *like* to be?"

"Hmm. The latter sounds more interesting."

"You know, I've never been to Yellowstone."

I give him a look. "You could pick anywhere, and it's *Wyoming*?"

"I'm not much of a Bahamas fellow, I suppose."

"You've heard of Paris, right?"

"Still a bit of a shambles there, actually."

"New York City?"

"For what?"

"Broadway, for one thing."

"Is that where you'd go?" he asks. "Broadway?"

"Buy two tickets to *Annie Get Your Gun* and your answer is yes."

He eases the car across the street and waves at the family as we pass. "Well, assuming we won't be in time to make the show in New York tonight, what's our next stop?"

I don't want to answer him—not because I don't have a firm idea of our destination, but because I'd rather be talking about Wyoming. Or wherever.

"So…?"

"Sorry." I point toward the river. "Back to the warehouse. We should warn Jesse Imada that he might be getting visitors."

"Got it." He turns a quick corner, shifts gears, and I stare out the passenger's window in the direction of somewhere else.

****

Somewhere else is not this dilapidated building in the muddy weeds on the edge of the city. *Somewhere else* is not under this harsh July sun. For the first time since my darkest days a few years ago, when so much was lost, I project myself into a future where I am not working the switchboard and sleeping in oversized clothes.

"Mrs. Frisco?"

I look away from the riverbank to find Derek watching me. "You don't have to call me that, you know."

He gives a faint grin. "Can I blame my military manners?"

"We've been through enough, you and I. 'Vivian' will do nicely."

He nods. "Pleased to meet you, Vivian. I'm Derek."

"Of course. Of O'Brien Engineworks, yes?"

He smiles. "The one and the same."

We approach the warehouse door as we did one week ago, noting the trampled grass and other signs of recent passage. The cigarette butts are layered in the soil, like strata in rock. If we could read them, what stories would they reveal? The temperature is already up to almost ninety degrees, the sun reflecting sharply off the windows high up in the walls.

I know something is wrong even before we open the door. The scent is too strong. It's the smell I remember—incense and brewing tea—but it's too potent, like a song on a radio turned up too loudly.

Derek reaches for the latch, but I stop him with a shake of my head. I'm not sure what to do or what we'll find inside.

He looks at me: *What's the matter?*

In reply, I shape my thumb and index finger into a gun.

That's all it takes. Derek slightly transforms, the way I imagine he does in the cockpit when he lets his reflexes take control of the stick. He slips the Sauer from his pocket. Moving lightly and almost entirely without sound, he touches the door handle, then gives it a gentle twist.

I stand behind him.

He swings open the door, the pistol held low but pointed inside.

No one is here.

The expansive space has been hastily evacuated.

Scattered across the floor are objects left behind like footprints: a few paperback books, spilled tea, some flatware, three pieces of sheet music, a shoe. Several potted plants sit abandoned on the shelves, two ferns and a collection of wandering Jews, their beautiful striped leaves long and well-tended and almost touching the ground. The tea service is gone, and so too are the racks of clothing and boxes of belongings the families had brought with them on their forced exodus to Kansas City. Incense-scented candles have burned all the way down to stubs, globs of wax hardened around then. Standing alone in the center of the room is the table where I sat with Jesse Imada and drank his tea. All that remains on the table is a single origami owl. Jesse asked about my *ikigai*—my reason for getting up in the morning and engaging with the world. I had no answer for him then.

"What happened here?" Derek asks. His voice sounds unusually small.

I say it with my face but not my words: This is my fault. I brought them here, the men who did this, the ones who drove the refugees away.

Derek shakes his head in gentle admonishment, but he must at least somewhat agree because he doesn't argue, just sets about walking the warehouse perimeter, though both of us can clearly see there's nothing left to find.

I kneel quietly and pick up the book. It is a well-handled copy of *Brave New World*.

The worst things here are the footprints.

When I visited before, I took off my shoes. The refugees wore only socks or went barefoot when indoors. I don't know why. But it was nice. Now, though…now the floor is covered in dirt smudges from the boots of the men who invaded this sacred family space. There must have been half a dozen of them. If I was any kind of actual, decent detective, I could follow these tracks directly back to their lair or hideout and—and what?

"Beat the shit out of them."

"Say again?" Derek asks from the far side of the warehouse.

"Nothing. I'm sorry."

"This isn't your fault."

I place the book on the table beside the paper owl. What would Kaz think of me, now that I've destroyed this haven he'd arranged?

Derek approaches. My eyes are closed, so I hear him instead of see him, sense him, read him with what I once boasted to Corky was extrasensory perception, but if I really was a mind-reader and not a charlatan, then those refugees wouldn't be searching for somewhere to shelter tonight.

"Hey."

I open my eyes.

"Kathy Mack's place isn't open on Sundays, so I can't distract you with dinner."

"That's fine, because I don't have much of an appetite."

"But I have another idea."

"Sorry, the bars are closed, too."

He doesn't smile. But there's an ember in his blue eyes. "I know one place that's always open. Come on. There's nothing else we can do here."

I let him lead me away to wherever the hell we're going, because he's right—there's not a damn thing I can do.

Chapter Twenty-Six

In Which I Eavesdrop

Beyond the city limits, every road is made of dirt. The state of Kansas is more important than you may know. We lead the nation in the production of wheat, in the number of newspapers per capita, and—oddly enough—in the amount of volcanic ash. We produce five times the mineral wealth of Alaska, and perhaps even more significantly, we are the geodetic center of the North American continent.

But our roads are terrible. Though our two-lane highways are mostly concrete or brick, once you turn onto a county thoroughfare, you're rolling on gravel or packed earth. The Cord was not constructed to navigate these lanes, yet we nonetheless find ourselves trundling slowly along, having abandoned Highway 50 for the open plains.

The top is down. I squint against the late-afternoon sun.

Derek and I haven't spoken for the last twenty minutes or so. He wisely lets the sunshine have its way with me. My anger subsides but doesn't depart. Like the rest of me, it's biding its time.

Derek eases to a stop in the middle of the road. There is no one else to be seen in any direction, just flat fields and a windmill in the distance. He shifts into neutral and leaves the big engine idling, then stares at me until I turn to face him.

"Fancy a go?" he asks.

"What are you talking about?"

He tips his head toward the steering wheel.

After a moment, I realize what he's suggesting. "Now?"

"You only live once."

"Yes, and I'd prefer not to end that life today by driving us into the ditch."

"You'd rather me take you home so you can sulk in silence?"

I raise my eyebrows in warning: *Don't go too far.*

He holds up a hand. "Easy. I just thought maybe you'd—"

"Fine." I swing open my door in a rush, plant my feet on the dirt, and circle the car.

Derek agilely slides over the shifter and into the passenger's seat.

I yank open the backward-facing door, drop into the driver's seat, and slam the door behind me. The steering wheel is white. The gauges on the aluminum console in front of me are polished to a sheen. I have no idea what oil pressure means.

"Do you…want instructions?"

I scoot forward in the seat and find the pedals. Last night, men entered my home uninvited and looked through my belongings. They were likely searching for Helena Crenshaw's stolen ballots. They will probably come looking again.

"Vivian?"

"Yes, please."

He tells me what I already know. But knowing it and

doing it are distant cousins, twice removed. I manage to get the car into gear. It shifts smoothly, forgivingly. The engine wants to go. It's sending me a message, a hum in my hand through the shift knob like the Morse code I learned about in Cordet's shop all those days ago.

"Ease off the clutch as you push down the accelerator."

Sure, I know that. My left hand grips the twelve-o'-clock spot on the wheel. The rearview mirror is mounted on the dashboard. No one is behind us. The dirt road in front of us is empty and rolls out to the horizon.

"Whenever you're ready."

Derek doesn't realize it, but he's summed up life right there in a single phrase. The days don't move at all until you're ready to make them go. If you never give the word, everything remains the same.

I lift my left foot in the same increments as I depress my right, and with no further encouragement required, the supercharged Cord Phaeton picks up speed.

"Steady as she goes." Derek settles back into his seat.

I am driving. The wind blows over the windshield and tosses my hair.

"Try the next gear."

I throw a glance at the shifter. A pattern of numbered grooves is built into it. I look back at the road, my fingers tight on the wheel, and I repeat the motion of the pedals as I move the stick.

The transmission grinds a little. I can feel Derek wince beside me. On the second try I get it right, and the car gathers more gasoline and turns it into fire.

No one is coming. The road is clear and leads somewhere west I've never been. Perhaps it will take us all the way to Wyoming if I keep going.

"She's got more in her," Derek says.

Is he talking about the car or me? I return to the gears. My timing is bad but my beginner's luck gets me through. At some point I dare a peek at the speedometer. We're doing almost sixty on a road designed for half that in a car that could easily double it.

I put both hands on the wheel and release the breath I've been holding. A quick glance at Derek reveals him to be leaning one elbow out of the window and smiling like a pool hustler.

Then I forget about him and everything else and simply drive.

****

On the way back home, I need to stop at Corky's house and tell him about the men in my house last night. Those ballots might exonerate Corky's client, Oliver Bishop, but they could also implicate someone else. Either way, their appearance before a court will invalidate the election results, which puts millions of pari-mutuel betting dollars at risk. A lot of people on both sides of the law are invested in the fate of what's currently residing in Corky's office safe.

Derek has resumed control of the car. We said little during the exchange. If he'd been trying to make some kind of point by having me drive, I suppose he made it, but the same can be said of me. I almost asked him if O'Brien Engineworks would employ female drivers one day, but the silence between us was too comfortable to interrupt.

We pull into the same spot at the curb where we parked for the dinner party the night before. Corky's sedan is not in the driveway. I don't know where he might be on a Sunday evening, but I'll leave word with Betty for him to give me a call.

We get out and head up the walk.

Corky attended Kansas State Teachers College in Emporia, which is evident in the collection of colorful ceramic hornets lining the flowerbeds below the windows. No football games have been played for the last several years, when our lives were suspended for the war, so Corky and everyone else are excited about the upcoming season. The soil looks freshly turned, so I assume he's been working outdoors today.

As I'm approaching the front door with its pretty eucalyptus wreath, Betty's voice carries through the glass, "...won't be back for at least another hour...yes, but let's not tempt fate, shall we?"

I can tell by her one-sided dialogue that Betty is on the telephone. I imagine her sitting in that floral-print parlor chair they bought at that new furniture store this spring, probably still wearing her church clothes from this morning but not her shoes.

"...certainly, you know me too well..."

We reach the door, the thrill of my recent drive still moving through me. I don't suspect I'll be purchasing an automobile anytime soon, but you never know. For the last two weeks, nothing has been predictable.

"You don't think Mr. Diantonio will say anything?"

I stop with my hand an inch from knocking. I'm not sure why.

"Why, he's Italian, for one. I'm not sure anyone trusts the Italians right now."

I remain still, listening to Betty's conversation.

"Well, I suppose he can use twenty dollars just like the rest of us."

I blame my hesitation on the strangeness of the day. What started with theft from government property led to driving without a license and from there to spying on my friend.

"Yes, yes, I'll stop being a nervous Nellie and let you—"

I knock.

Betty's voice drops. I don't hear her say goodbye or hang up, but seconds later she opens the door.

We smile at the same time. Mine is automatic and not entirely authentic, and I suspect hers is the same. She wears no cosmetics at this hour, certainly not expecting any company, and I decide immediately that I appreciate her like this. She's more real than on those afternoons she invites me over for tea.

"Well, Vivian!" She raises her eyebrows. "What on earth?"

"Sorry I didn't call."

She looks at Derek. "Mr. O'Brien."

"Good evening."

"Is Corky home?" I ask.

"Not currently, no. Is something wrong?"

"It's about a case."

"On a Sunday evening?"

"I apologize. But we wanted to let him know that a third party is interested in the materials we transferred to him two days ago."

"I don't understand."

"Can you give him the message?"

"Vivian, I have no idea what you're talking about. If you'd let me know you were coming over—"

"Will you tell him? This matter involves one of his clients."

"And it couldn't wait until the morning?"

"I'm afraid not."

"Well…" She waves a hand vaguely. "Would the two of you like to come in and wait for him? I'll need to freshen up first, but—"

"We're fine, Betty. We just need for him to know. Could you have him telephone me when he's back?"

"Yes, yes, of course."

"Thank you."

"This is all highly irregular, you know. My husband doesn't make a habit of bringing his work home with him."

"It's an important case."

"I'm sure it is."

"Thank you again."

She nods. We wish each other goodnight. Derek gives her a nod and a "Mrs. Schneider" in way of benediction, and then the door is closed and we're standing on the porch as dusk turns into night.

I stare into the street, tapping my fingernail against my chin.

"What is it?" Derek asks.

"What do you mean?"

"You have a look."

"Do I?" Before he says anything else, I head to the car, keeping my thoughts to myself.

Chapter Twenty-Seven

In Which I Pay a Bribe

I attend class on Monday morning as if none of this is happening. I sit in my usual third-row seat in a medium-sized lecture hall at U of M's campus on Holmes Street, copying notes from a blackboard that is cloudy with chalk. The textbook open in front of me, roughly the size and density of the Gutenberg Bible, is titled *Fundamentals of Criminal Law and Court Procedures*. Apparently the authors have only a passing familiarity with paragraph breaks and no faith at all in illustrations.

For the next few hours I try to put everything out of my mind and be a dutiful student.

By early afternoon I'm back at work. The day moves in predictable segments, frustratingly ordinary. I perform the functions of my job automatically, more like a robot in a pulp magazine than a person. By now the Agawa family has likely lost all faith in Vivian-san. I have sorted through all avenues of further inquiry but have found only dead ends. If either Wallace Breckenridge or his caddy Arlen Dunkirk are responsible for what happened to Kaz, I don't know what else I can do to prove it. I sense there's something I'm overlooking, but I can't quite capture it because one particular phrase Betty used last night keeps distracting me:

...won't be back for at least another hour...

My grammar teacher would have called that a sentence fragment. As to where Corky might have been and why Betty would have assured someone about his arrival time, well, there are probably close to a dozen explanations, each more mundane than the last. But ever since the second of July, when all of this began, I've been seeing hobgoblins in every shifting shadow, no matter how normal that shadow might seem.

Ergo, this happens:

Between calls, I open the index and—with a practiced swiftness—find the name "Diantonio" before Ms. Peele realizes I'm freelancing again.

There are two listings. One is for a woman named Idabell and the other a man named Franklin. Betty had said *mister*, so I return the index in time to take the next call, pulling a cable from a socket and plugging it in somewhere else. The fact that I'm planning to snoop on my dear friend is one more sign that I'm taking all of this too far. As if stealing the gun wasn't enough.

****

I call Franklin Diantonio as soon as I'm home. Derek offered to drive me after work, but I told him I needed the walk to sort my thoughts. Kansas City on a summer evening is not so bad a place, really. Nat Looper told me he spotted no uninvited visitors while I was away, he being my omnipresent sentinel on the corner. Hopefully in the meantime Corky moved the stolen ballots to a different location, just in case.

Satchel leaps into my lap as the line rings in my ear.

A man's voice answers, "Tuscany Lane Motor Court."

I do not know what to say to this. I was expecting

"Diantonio residence," or perhaps the increasingly popular "Hello," but instead it's the name of a business.

"Is anyone there?"

"I'm sorry, I—what are your operating hours?" It's the only thing I can manage that sounds like a logical reason for calling.

"Ma'am, we're proud to be open twenty-four hours a day. If you're on the road and in need of a night's boarding, Tuscany Court is the only lodging available on Route Fifty." He says it in a practiced manner, the words like a radio jingle.

"Uh, thank you. I'll keep that in mind." I return the receiver to the cradle.

It rings immediately and scares the shit out of me.

The cat leaps away. I recover by the third ring. "Good evening, Vivian speaking."

"I hope it's not too late for a call, dearie."

"Helena?"

"Is this a bad time?"

My pulse settles. I exhale and look around, suddenly nervous. What if the intruders had avoided Nat's observing eye? Or what if they'd paid him off and are even now gliding up the stairs? How trustworthy is he, after all?

"Are you still with me?"

"Yes, I'm here."

"I won't keep you. I was just wondering if you'd care for lunch tomorrow?"

"Lunch?"

"Yes, you know, the meal held at midday between breakfast and dinner. Would you care to meet up? I don't cook, of course, but there's a French sous chef in town who owes me a favor."

"Um…"

"I forbid you to say no."

"Helena, it's just that I…"

"You don't eat lunch?"

"I do."

"Of course you do. I'll pick you up. See you at quarter till noon." She ends the call.

I hold the phone against my ear. If I could crawl into the receiver and wiggle through the wires, I would eventually emerge at a certain switchboard, where the girl working the shift after mine would connect me to anywhere in the world I wanted to go—anywhere at all. The notion is a strange one. But it doesn't feel so unreasonable, all things considered.

I keep the receiver in place, dial the switchboard, and request to be routed to Uncle Charlie's number. If strangeness is the order of the day, then I'll embrace it and ask Derek if he has anything better to do on a muggy Monday night than visit a motor court with rooms to rent on Highway Fifty.

****

Our conversation on the ride to speak with Mr. Diantonio is an exchange of questions, like an odd tennis match where neither of us can quite see the net.

"…but how does this motor court figure into the murder?" Derek asks as he drives.

"Did I say the two events are somehow connected?"

"Isn't that what you implied?"

"Who do you think Betty was talking to last night?"

"Are you assuming she has something to hide?"

"Did you hear her wonder if Mr. Diantonio could keep a secret?"

"You're sure she used that exact word?"

I don't immediately reply. No, I'm not sure, actually. But she certainly said something along those lines. I stare up at the dark sky. This morning the news broadcaster said that Venus would be visible tonight in the constellation of Leo, currently some 102 million miles away. I know nothing of astronomy, but I remember that Venus was the goddess of beauty and love.

"What do you think about Helena Crenshaw?" I ask without looking away from the stars.

"What of her?"

"Do you think she's lonely?"

"How would I know that, exactly?"

"What was your assessment after meeting her?"

"I'm not the one she's asking out for lunch, remember?"

"Does that bother you?" Earlier I told him about my appointment with Helena tomorrow afternoon. He advised me to be careful—of what, precisely, I'm still not certain. "What do you think Kaz knew that got him killed?"

"Haven't we been over this before?"

"What have I overlooked?"

"Can we finally agree that maybe the police are right and he was murdered by a racist passerby?"

"Is that what you really think happened?"

"Why are you asking so many questions?"

"Would you like me to stop?"

"Could you, please?"

Derek can't see it, but I smile at him in the dark. I think about giving him a mischievous poke in the ribs, but that feels like it might be crossing a line. I content myself with stargazing, hunting around for Leo, the lion of the night sky.

****

Few things are more American than a roadside motor court. Take a few small cottages, provide adequate parking and a proprietor who answers the bell at any hour of the day, and you end up with waystations along the country's ever-expanding highway system. We the people are free of the war and free of the fascists and free of gasoline rations. Thanks to new money for infrastructure and new incentives to explore, each road now connects to another, and if you're going to navigate to the places you see on postcards, you need a pillow along the way on which to rest your head.

The Tuscany Lane Motor Court consists of half a dozen little buildings painted green with white trim, their rooflines adorned in a faux Florentine style. They share access to a croquet court of neatly trimmed grass, illuminated by gas-powered lamps. Derek parks near a barrel of croquet mallets, and we walk toward a hand-painted sign reading PULL BELL FOR SERVICE ANYTIME—GRAZIE! The Italians surrendered almost three years ago, so by now apparently it's fine to speak the language again.

"Your leave's almost over," I say to him without really knowing why.

"So it is. Life as a fighter pilot will seem positively boring after all of this."

"Well, I'll drop you a line from time to time to remind you of all you're missing."

"I'd like that. Assuming the mail arrives, that is."

We stop before the door and its drawstring bell. "The Air Corps has trouble with the postal service?"

"You'd be amazed by what doesn't function

properly in the military." He gives the string a sharp pull.

You'd think by now I'd be better at waiting. I am not.

The door opens just before Derek can give a second tug. Illuminated from behind, the man who greets us reminds me of one of my law professors, with gray in his eyebrows and an unremarkable necktie. "Evening, folks. Welcome to Tuscany Lane."

Derek removes his hat. "We're happy to be here."

For a moment I see the two of us through the innkeeper's eyes, and suddenly we are not us at all but entirely different people: a not-quite-youthful couple with a brazen car, driving across the country on summer vacation, weary from the road, the gleam of California in our tired smiles. I pull this persona around myself like a cloak and say, "We're hoping you have a vacancy."

"Surely I do, ma'am. Please come in."

He holds the door open for us, then follows us inside, moving behind the counter as I take in the kitschy Italian décor.

"So where you folks driving in from?"

"Back east," Derek replies without hesitation.

"Do you see a lot of business here?" I ask him.

"Yes, ma'am, in the summer we're blessed to meet travelers from all over this great country of ours. You're lucky to find us with an empty bed."

I pass my eyes over the open ledger in front of him. "I've never stayed the night at a motor court before. What's the process?"

"Couldn't be simpler, ma'am. All you need to do is sign in and pay for your stay in advance, and I hand over the key." He smiles.

"We sign in?" Derek asks.

"As a new security precaution, yes sir. A lot of Germans have been coming over and living under assumed names."

"So I've heard."

"I don't want any Nazis sleeping under my roof."

"Of course not."

"I make it a point to check everyone's credentials. I apologize for the inconvenience, but I'll need to see your license to drive, sir."

Derek waves a hand to say that it's no trouble at all. "Just last week I read that the Boston police found a Gestapo officer trying to get a job as a schoolteacher. Can you imagine?" He withdraws his wallet as the two men move from Boston war criminals to Boston athletics, namely professional football, with the struggling Yanks having selected a quarterback from Notre Dame as the first overall pick in the draft.

"Not sure if *any* player is going to save that poor team," the innkeeper says.

"You're probably right, friend."

I paid my first bribe only nine nights ago when I convinced the guard at the boxing matches to allow us backstage. Perhaps corrupted by that experience, I extract two twenty-dollar bills from my handbag. The room rates here are two dollars per night. I put almost three weeks' worth atop the open ledger. "Do you mind giving us a few minutes?"

The innkeeper holds my gaze, drums his fingers twice, then takes the money with a nod. "If you don't mind, I need to check the public toilet facilities out back. We just had the plumbing installed, so no more outhouses for our guests."

Derek nods. "Of course."

"You folks are in bungalow number two. Sometimes you have to jiggle the light to get it to come on." He puts a key on the countertop and leaves us alone.

As soon as he's gone, I slide the ledger closer and use my fingertip to scan the names.

The page is divided into three columns. The date appears in the first, the patron's name in the second, and a checkmark in the last designates whether or not the bill has been paid in full. The quality of the penmanship ranges from the meticulous and legible to the slapdash and borderline hieroglyphic. As such, I don't read the names so much as wait for the recognizable to jump off the page. But my finger reaches the bottom margin without snagging on an obvious SCHNEIDER. There is no indication that Betty was here.

Derek stands beside me like a lookout as I return to the top of the page and start again, paying more attention this time, hoping to tease some instant meaning from the litany of names. I can't help but wonder about these people as I briefly encounter them. Who, exactly, are Mr. and Mrs. Kenneth Coltrane, and where were they headed when they spent a balmy evening here in late June? They sound adventuresome, those Coltranes, Ken a young corporal back from Calais, his wife a French schoolteacher he convinced to marry him and run off to the States and start a family. Or Sven Olsen, who stayed here a few days later, a Danish widower spending the last part of his summer on tour of the Midwest before returning to life as a literature professor back in Maine. My imagination breathes life into them as they pass below my finger.

I see a name I recognize and stop.

The ledger says E. SKINNER rented a cottage three

days ago. I know two Skinners, of course, Gene and Darb, with whom we ate dinner at Corky's place on Saturday. Across America there are likely thousands of Skinners, so this one might refer to Ernie or Ezekial, or perhaps to an Everett Skinner from Minot, North Dakota, who was in town for the bachelor party of his roommate from college.

"Or Eugene."

"Come again?" Derek asks.

I lift my eyes from the book, finger still in place, moving the possibility through my mind.

"What is it?"

"Gene's full name is probably Eugene."

"Gene Skinner spent the night here?"

"Possibly. Or maybe just a few hours."

"Correct me if I'm wrong, but it sounds like you're accusing your friend Betty of..."

Derek doesn't finish his thought, but I'm already far ahead of him, weighing the *what ifs* and wondering how she could do that to Corky. I assume the worst because that's what we do, we humans, stealing peeks over the backyard fence and hoping to catch a glimpse of something worth talking about at the hair salon. *Betty has been unfaithful to her husband.* This is the same husband who spent the last several years liberating Europe, whose disloyalty to his wife went no further than gawking at a passed-around pinup of the latest Vargas girl.

"Vivian?"

It can't be true. I overheard half a conversation and found one signature in a book. The future lawyer in me would call that circumstantial evidence, at best.

"What's our next move?" he asks.

"We leave, I suppose."

"Come along then. We should make ourselves scarce before we overstay our time here with confidential records." Derek sets the room key on the ledger and slides it back across the counter. "It'll be the easiest forty bucks the man's ever made."

"Sure." I give the key a glance, my eyes falling on it at the same time as Derek's. "He won't even need to clean the room after we're gone."

"Nope," Derek agrees.

A moment passes. The key to bungalow number two glimmers on the countertop. I don't have any idea what to do.

In the beginning, God created the heavens and the earth. So begins the most famous story of all. Does my own story start here, turning upon that cottage key as if it were the pivot point of my life? Or did it already begin two weeks ago when I resolved to avenge Kaz's ghost, like some ill-prepared understudy in a Shakespearean play? It feels different than it used to, this life of mine.

I allow myself to smile. It's real and warm and will chart its own course. "Let's go. Maybe you can let me drive."

It takes him a second, then he nods. "You bet, but do you really think driving in the dark is a good idea?"

I don't answer him. There are too many competing voices in my heart.

Chapter Twenty-Eight

In Which I Am Threatened

On the front page of the Tuesday morning *Star* is an ominous warning: STRIKE SHUTS OFF BEER. Apparently picket lines at the city's two largest breweries have been formed because the owners can't give the union workers a five-dollar-per-week raise due to decreased revenues, which they blame on the lack of sufficient malt supplies. Without malt, there's no beer, and without beer, the hard-working people of Kansas City might raze the mayor's office if he doesn't intervene.

After checking the box scores—the Monarchs are still leading the league, with twenty-three wins and thirteen losses—I push the paper away and think about Betty and Gene.

Perhaps it would be easier to understand in baseball terms. I spent the night angry at both of them, feeling betrayed on Corky's behalf, and the cluster of those emotions makes it impossible to accept the truth. But put a runner in scoring position, with a three-two count, and maybe I can make sense of it.

The catcher gives a sign between his legs. The pitcher replies with an almost imperceptible nod. He moves his eyes barely at all, a glance at the runner on third and the daringly long lead he's taken from the bag.

Or she. Because that runner is me. I'm almost home, but not quite yet. If Gene Skinner's on the mound and he's trading secret information with Betty behind the plate, then I'm obliged to try and intercept the signs. I remember the two of them in the kitchen together on Saturday night while the rest of us were sipping drinks. I recall almost every word of Betty's phone conversation, overheard through her wreath-decorated door. And there was Gene renting a room when his house is only fifteen minutes away.

Sudden laughter from the downstairs apartment pulls me from my dark place. I listen, but there's nothing more. The floor is thin, and sometimes the joy of being in love bubbles up from the bedroom of the couple below. I resolve to introduce myself to them when all of this is through.

I'm scheduled for lunch with Helena and then work from two until ten. That leaves little time for seething about Betty or wondering about Kaz, which means I'm going to continue a disturbing trend and call in sick this afternoon. Ms. Peele won't tolerate many more of those. But, entirely out of options though not yet willing to admit defeat to the Agawa family, I have to do the one desperate thing remaining:

I must return to the scene of the crime.

****

"…and then Gregory Peck says to her, 'I take it this is your first honeymoon.'"

"And then what happens?" I ask between bites of my *croque monsieur.*

"She says something romantic back and they kiss, of course. It's wonderful and completely preposterous. Couples don't talk like that in real life."

"What happens at the end?"

Helena waves with her fork. "Oh, the murderer gets exposed, shoots himself, and the two improbably good-looking leads ride off into the celluloid sunset."

"I'm sorry I missed that one." We're enjoying an early lunch in the small dining area of her apartment above Family Investment Capital. Every window is open in an effort to capture a possible breeze, but the room remains warm, and soon I'm likely to be sweating into my printed seersucker brunch coat, pink with navy dots. Helena arranged for a local chef to drop by, rather than having us visit a restaurant in person, and when I ask why, she says, "People talk, dearie."

"What people?"

"The kind who can't mind their own business."

"Two women eating fancy ham sandwiches is gossip-worthy?"

"When one of those women is me, yes, it can sometimes be. I wouldn't want any of that rubbing off on you." She smiles at me, but in the lines around her eyes, I see an old pain.

We talk about my law studies and about my cat. We talk about her time as a governess for a New England family and of her weakness for vanilla taffy. On the small table between us is a stoneware mortar she claims is from an archeological dig in Macedonia, and I see no reason to doubt her. The mortar is full of salt, which she uses liberally on her eggs.

"So tell me about your future law firm," she says, dabbing her lips. "Do you plan to practice here in town or somewhere more sensible, like San Francisco?"

"I think I'm a long way from having to make that decision. I have to get through my coursework, and at some point a hundred years from now, I'll need to pass the bar examination."

"You've never thought about it? Don't lie to me now. I know a daydreamer when I see one."

"Well, I plan on having indoor cooling, wherever I end up."

"May we all, one day! With practical sensibilities like that, I'm sure you'll end up on the Supreme Court."

I allow myself a laugh. "Do they allow women?"

"There has to be a first, dearie, and it might as well be you."

She asks me more questions that people don't usually ask. I find myself shaping my answers in a way that makes me sound more interesting than I actually am. We pass an hour that way, a lively back and forth that forces me to divulge pieces of myself, the way one pushes open a door slightly stuck in the jamb.

She starts to ask me about Derek but, outside the open windows, a horn honks three times. Then twice more.

Frowning, Helena stands up to investigate, and because curiosity has become my tailwind recently, I follow her and look down from the big window, not knowing what to expect. These days it could be anything.

A black Buick Super idles in the middle of the street. Standing beside it in the sun are two men in suits— probably the very two who searched my home.

They're looking straight up at us. "Afternoon, ladies."

Helena puts her hands on the sill and leans out. "What do you want?"

"A certain civil servant by the name of Pietro Modani gave something to you."

"Get lost."

The man's a little stoop-shouldered, his coat sleeves too short for his arms. His partner stands beside him and smokes. "We're here to collect a bit of merchandise that Modani gave you by mistake."

"Who sent you?"

I know the answer to this one. "They work for the man with the shovel."

Helena shoots me a glance, frowning, then looks back down at the men.

"That doesn't matter," he says, his voice carrying easily, causing a few folks on the sidewalk to glance over. "We'll be back here at one minute till midnight tonight and take that package off your hands. That gives you almost twelve hours."

"And what if I fail to answer your polite knock?"

"That's up to you. We know you took possession of the merchandise. We know you haven't involved the authorities." He nods at me. "We know you're friendly with Jim Frisco's widow there."

I am struck by a compelling desire to flip him the bird. I resist.

Helena crosses her arms over her chest. "Can't say I know what you're talking about. Sorry, but you have the wrong *femme fatale*."

"Whatever you say, Ms. Crenshaw. Either way, we'll be knocking on your door at one minute till midnight."

"Is that a threat?"

"No, but this is. You two hand over those ballots tonight or we'll burn this shithole down to the root cellar." They climb into the Buick and yank its big doors shut.

We watch them drive away.

"Assholes," Helena says.

"I'm afraid they're serious."

"Of course they're serious." She turns to look at me. Once again the lines around her eyes reveal her, like runes of the woman within. This time I see fear. "Has your lawyer friend handed that box to the police?"

"Last I knew, the ballots are still locked in his office safe."

She nods, tightens her arms around herself, and looks off into the direction of the disappearing car.

Chapter Twenty-Nine

In Which I Discover a Locked Door

That ruins lunch. We leave our plates sitting there, our meal unfinished, most of our stories untold. Helena has changed clothes, perhaps sensing that trousers will be more practical for whatever the day may bring. She's dressed like an adventuress from an English travelogue, albeit one slightly anxious around the edges.

I use her telephone—an oval-shaped Model 202 from the 1930s—to dial the switchboard and get connected to Uncle Charlie, who answers on the third ring and informs me immediately that he's running a sale on complete oil changes and that he'll beat any price in town. I tell him it's me, he sounds honestly pleased to hear my voice, and I give him as much small talk as possible while Helena pulls on a different pair of shoes. I ask him if his nephew is available, and he says Derek is out waxing his car, because of course he is.

"Tell him to meet me at Corky Schneider's office."

"That doesn't sound like a request."

"Not this time."

"Hey, you know he ships out pretty soon, right?"

"Unfortunately, yes."

"You two in some kind of trouble?"

"I can't really say."

"You can't say because you *are*?"

"Maybe. Can you just tell him, please?"

"Sure thing, kiddo. Old Uncle Charlie's never done you wrong."

As soon as I hang up, Helena says, "Hell of a mess for a perfectly good Tuesday."

I gently return the receiver to its cradle, professionally respectful of the hardware. "Hell of a one, indeed."

****

If you're driving through Kansas City at midday, and if it happens to be midday in the summer, and if that summer happens to be this one, then you crank every window down so as not to perish of heat stroke, but you discover that superheated air blowing through the car is almost worse than none at all. The newspapers occasionally talk about companies that will install weather conditioners in your vehicle, but I have never seen one.

Helena shifts gears as we turn left at a busy intersection. She knows the city as well as I do, can sense its pulse. "So he's teaching you to drive?"

I've already grown accustomed to her habit of using pronouns without antecedents. You're just supposed to figure out the *he* or *it* to which she is referring. "I'm afraid the teacher has more enthusiasm than the pupil."

"Driving is not an activity for the timid."

"You know, I read a book on it once."

"A book on what?"

"How to drive."

"Did it help?"

"I thought it needed more diagrams. I'm still not entirely sure what the choke does."

"So the two of you are…business partners?"

"I don't have a business. For that matter, neither does he. But he plans to own a racing outfit one day."

"Automobile racing? They never grow up, these boys we call men."

For some reason, this reminds me of Ace Norris, my teenage sweetheart. I've not seen him since he moved away, so in my mind, he'll forever be a boy, faultless, with Mercury's wings tied to his heels. "Maybe that's not always a bad thing."

"By now you know that I'm not afraid of asking personal questions without permission."

I look out the open window, the wind throwing my hair into disarray, and smile to myself. "The answer is no."

"No what?"

"No, Mr. O'Brien and I are not involved."

"Well, you're sure involved in *something*."

"So are you, it would seem."

"Yes, I suppose that's what I get for entrusting a lawyer's pretty assistant with stolen property. I should have kept those ballots in hiding and let the world move on without my interference."

The lawyer's assistant, for her part, stares from the window at the rushing city, the afternoon shoppers browsing the storefronts, the policeman on his beat. Over the years, I've visited most of those businesses for one reason or another. I recognize more than a few faces. I feel as if I've grown into this town, the way a girl eventually grows into a woman's gown. Perhaps because I don't own a car and have spent the better part of recent years on foot, moving from one street to the next, the city has taken pity on me, adopted me, raised me in its own image—for whatever that's worth.

"Can I ask you something, dearie?"

I turn to look at her.

"After this is over, assuming we survive the night and all, do you suppose we could pick up where we left off at lunch?"

"We'll see. I don't think I should make any more promises until I do right by the ones I've already made."

"That's a fair answer."

We ride those last few blocks in silence to the former office of Schneider & Frisco Investigations, where stolen property is hidden and a good man died.

Two weeks ago, it began like this:

A switchboard worker and part-time law student walked into a building lobby. She had been there many times before, most often at the noon hour to share sandwiches and pie with her husband and his partner. The war ended that tradition as it had ended so many others. Later she resumed her visits, more guarded and less everything else. A small payment from the government in recognition of her loss was just enough for college tuition. One day, like any other day, she'd stopped by and greeted the custodian who'd been here before dawn.

Morning, ma'am.

Hello, Kaz. Is he in?

Since sunrise.

What? Why so early?

Big case, maybe? Or wife kicked him out?

Betty Schneider has never kicked anyone in her life. She wears nice shoes.

Shoes that expensive should be a crime.

The custodian is wise enough not to look down at the woman's shoes, which cost four dollars and change.

Have a good day, ma'am.

Hey, Kazuhiko?

Yes?

"Next time we meet," I whisper as Helena and I enter the lobby, "call me Vivian."

"Come again?"

"Just remembering." I move slowly, a swimmer underwater. Here is the place he stood when I asked him to call me by my given name, which is from the Latin word *vivus*, meaning *alive*. I am starting to feel that way again in recent days. Here is the place where his body came to rest, the tiles washed clean of blood, probably with the very mop he used every day. I move to the lobby's narrow broom closet and look inside: yes, there is a metal pail, a mop, and a wooden box of cleaning rags.

"Dearie?"

I turn and look past Helena at the front windows and the sidewalk beyond. The avenue is narrow here, unable to accommodate parked vehicles against the curb. That's why the police cars that morning were parked in the street.

I turn to Helena. "The person who killed Kaz didn't park a car out front."

"All right. So what does that mean?"

"They would have been forced to leave it idling in the street, and that would have drawn too much attention."

"You're saying they parked around the corner and walked in?"

"No, for the same reason. They would have been seen walking around the building and then out again. It would be too risky. It's busy around here in the mornings. Someone would almost certainly have seen them."

"I'm afraid I'm lost, then."

I glance at the door to Corky's office. It's slightly ajar. He's inside and expecting us but doesn't yet know we've arrived. I move across the lobby, to the opposite side near the stairs. Helena follows. I wonder if Derek is on his way. I'm sure he is. I can almost hear the Cord's engine change octaves as he shifts gears.

I stop in front of an oak door set deep into the rear wall. The hand-painted letters are faded but legible: EXIT. "This leads outside."

"Sure. So there's parking out back?"

"Yes, but this door isn't used by the public. It stays locked." To demonstrate, I grab the tarnished brass knob and give a twist; it moves but the door holds fast.

"I'll say it again. I'm lost."

"Whoever killed Kaz came in through this door. It's the only other way inside."

"They picked the lock?"

"Or?"

She narrows her eyes, thinks about it, and says, "Or they had a key?"

"*Or?*"

"What is this, a radio quiz show?"

"Or someone let them in."

"Right. I guess it could be any one of those things. So which one?"

"Viv?" Corky stands in his office doorway across the lobby, cigarette between his thumb and forefinger. "Everything okay?"

Helena looks from me to the doorknob and back again. "You haven't answered my question. Which one?"

"I'm not sure, but I'm almost there. Come on." My shoes have always sounded too loud on this floor; they sounded that way years ago when I was walking to the lair of a private eye, and they sound that way now when it has become an attorney's den. Everything has changed except the cadence of my heels on the tile.

"You two weren't followed?" Corky asks.

"Would we know it if we were?"

"These guys you mentioned on the telephone, would you be able to describe them?"

"Are we going to the police with that information?"

"You have a better idea?"

"Maybe." I brush past him and enter the office. "Let's talk."

Chapter Thirty

In Which I Count Keys

The minute hand of Corky's wall clock hits 1:59,
which gives us exactly ten hours. Derek has arrived, and
his sudden appearance in the office doorway catches me
mid-sentence. He wears dark chinos and a white linen
shirt open at the throat that reveals the V of his upper
chest, where his dog tags reside, the metal polished like
silver.

"What did I miss?" he asks.

I remember the moment I met him. Uncle Charlie
dispatched him to my door. He told me his name and then
introduced me to his car.

I motion to the chair beside me. "Have a seat." The
four of us fill up Corky's modest office. He's opened all
the windows, one of them propped up with a wooden
ruler. He's positioned a fan on the windowsill, its metal
blades spinning to little avail.

Derek tips his head toward me. "Shouldn't you be at
work?"

"You're starting to sound suspiciously like Ms.
Peele."

He grins.

Corky leans forward, elbows on his desk. "This is
how I see the situation."

He begins to talk. He starts with taking on the

wrongfully accused Oliver Bishop as a client, but all I can think about is that his wife may have cheated on him. In a courtroom, they'd call my evidence circumstantial—an overheard telephone call, a signature in a motor court ledger—but I have a feeling that proof wouldn't be hard to find if I really went looking.

Do I want to go looking?

"...at which point Pietro Modani, the actual thief, asks Ms. Crenshaw here to hold onto the ballots, maybe for a rainy day or something."

"And it never rains but it pours," Helena says, fanning her face with a manila folder from Corky's desk.

"How did these guys find out you had the ballots?"

"I employ several people, not all of them entirely reputable."

"One of your own crew tipped them off?"

"That's not shocking, is it?"

"And these men are coming back tonight to collect?"

Derek shifts in his seat. "I haven't heard this part. What men? Did something happen this morning?"

Helena fills him in, embellishing only a few details, while I consider the locked door at the back of the lobby and who might hold the keys. Certainly Kaz had a key in his possession, as he was often the first in the building. Did he open that door after someone knocked? Did he know that person?

When Helena finishes her description of the encounter, complete with the warning to be ready with the ballots at one minute before midnight, Derek turns to me, the look on his face identical to the one he wore the moment we stole the gun. "This isn't safe any longer."

"It hasn't been safe for a while, I'm afraid."

"I think it's time to speak with the authorities."

Helena shakes her head. "Count me out, if that's the plan."

Corky taps ashes into a tin saucer. "I'd love to hand this mess over to the police, but I need the ballots to get my client off the hook."

I look at the safe in the corner. It is a squat black box about two feet high, a weathered Diebold model that I assume has been secured to the floor. It's probably fifty years old. I'm not sure if Corky purchased it or if Jim found it somewhere, but the safe has been here since their grand opening, which wasn't very grand. Two weeks passed before they got their first paying client.

Helena gives up on her makeshift fan, returning the folder to the top of the nearest pile. "Ollie Bishop being acquitted is far less important than preventing my livelihood from being burned down. Those ballots are being handed to the goons tonight, tied with pink ribbon if that's what they want."

Derek says, "I believe they're the property of the voters, aren't they?"

"Did you hear what I said? Those men are going to set a fire on my property, and they won't care who might be inside when it all goes up in flames. I might remind you that I live in that building."

"All the more reason to get the police involved."

"And you think they're going to protect me?" She makes a sound midway between a hiss and a laugh. "If I don't hand those ballots over to him, I'm going to have to leave town for good and never come back—and I'll spend the rest of my life hoping he doesn't find me."

"He who?"

Helena looks at me, eyebrows raised.

"The man with the shovel," I say.

"All right, all right." Corky waves us down with his cigarette. "We're all law-abiding citizens here, more or less, so we can't have it both ways. Before any of us leave this office, we need to decide if the ballots are going to the district attorney's office where they belong or to pay off whoever hired Modani to steal them in the first place."

Derek and Helena immediately swing back to their debate.

I lean closer to Corky's desk, turning it all over, wondering.

"What is it, Viv?"

"May I ask you a question?"

"Have I ever said no to that?"

"Who has a key to this building?"

It takes him a moment, then he smiles darkly while inhaling hard on his cigarette. "Jesus, we're back to the janitor again."

"Did he have a key?"

"Of course he had a key. He got here before I did, on most days."

"And every other office space is still empty?"

"Like a lot of other places around town, yeah. Thank the Fatherland for that one."

"And you have a key."

"Sure."

"Anyone else?"

"Well, the owner, I guess."

"Wallace Breckenridge?"

"The one and the same. Where are you going with this?"

"What if someone unlocked the door and let

themselves in that morning?"

"You got an awful lot of *what ifs* in you."

"More and more every day."

"Look, you know I think you're not going to get anywhere with this, but either way, let's table for it for now until we deal with the present situation. And I have two, actually."

"Two keys?"

He nods.

"Why two?"

He holds my gaze for the longest time. It's a look he hasn't given me in quite a while. After a moment, it makes sense. I say, softly, "You inherited Jim's key."

He reaches across the desk, gives my hand a brief squeeze. "We can figure that other stuff out later. Right now we need to resolve this ballot shit."

I pinch my lips shut for a second, then agree with a tip of my head. "All right. I may have a solution for this…this ballot shit."

He winks. "Why doesn't that surprise me?"

****

Al Capone is currently a free man. The papers say his mental health is declining rapidly. But he's living in a Florida mansion instead of Alcatraz, so there's that. During his trial for tax evasion, a witness said he was ordered by the gangster to get the money out of the house, in case the IRS showed up: "There was so much cash, I had to split it up into two bags. One bag went to his people in Chicago, the other to his people in New York. That day, everybody was happy to see me." The jury supposedly laughed

"We divide the ballots in two." I'm standing in front of one of the windows, a line of perspiration along the center of my back. "It's my belief that no one has any idea how many ballots were taken, not even Modani himself. I certainly haven't counted them. The authorities don't need to be given any particular number to suggest the illegitimacy of the election and to cast a shadow of doubt on their case against Mr. Bishop. The rest we present to the men in the black Buick, whatever number it takes to get them to go away."

I look around, waiting, watching their faces. The fan pushes a strand of hair in front of my face.

"Bravo, dearie." Helena claps a few times.

"It might satisfy all parties," Corky agrees.

I look at Derek. It occurs to me that the value I place on his opinion is not in balance with the number of days I've known him. His eyes haven't changed since hearing about the threat we received. If anything, he appears even more troubled. "Who will do the handover?"

"I'm sorry?"

"Someone's going to have to hand a hatbox of ballots to suspected criminals on a dark street. The situation will be unpredictable, at best. They'll be armed."

"What do you suggest?"

"Are we officially ruling out involving the police?"

"For now, yes."

"And you're confident these men will simply tip their hats to you and cause no more trouble once they have what they want?"

"Well…I suppose I was hoping you'd volunteer to come along."

"You know I will."

"We *all* will," Corky says.

"Speak for yourself," Helena says. "I'll be inside

with the shades drawn, thank you very much."

Our idea develops from there. Derek and I will wait on the walk in front of Helena's building, most of the ballots in one of Corky's old briefcases. Corky himself will be just inside the lobby, watching from the window. When the black Buick arrives, we'll pass over the case, and the men will depart back to whatever lair they call home, and we'll never see them again.

Or so goes the plan.

Chapter Thirty-One

In Which I Stand My Ground

Between the moment we adjourned from Corky's office until the second I stepped onto the dark sidewalk in front of Helena's building, this is what happened:

3:15 PM. Derek drives me home to change clothes. What was suitable attire for my lunch with Helena will not suffice for midnight assignations. Music lessons being conducted above the pastry shop across the street carry from their open windows to mine, and I change into a simple gray skirt and white blouse to a piano rendition of "It Had to Be You." We all know the song well enough by now that I whisper the lyrics to myself as I put on more businesslike shoes.

3:41. Derek exhibits gentlemanly patience, as I'm still sorting myself out behind my bedroom door.

3:52. I emerge refreshed to find Derek on the sofa with Satchel vying for his attention while he skims my copy of the latest *Pageant* magazine. Back at the switchboard, Ms. Peele—standing behind my empty stool—is probably wondering what's gotten into me.

3:56. I ask Nat Looper to keep an eye on the stairs to my apartment. He assures me that he'll hold the line. Derek transfers the briefcase to the Cord's trunk. Corky purchased that case the week he became a licensed investigator. It bears the marks of the intervening years.

I think about Betty as I slide into the seat, Derek closing the door behind me. Betty and Gene.

4:27. We arrive on campus to drop off my latest typed assignments and to check out from the library a book on my professor's list of suggested reading, and by suggested he means mandatory if one intends to pass the course. I sign my name on the library card and walk out with *A Post-War Judicial Review of Constitutional Freedoms and Statutory Executive Powers*, which sounds like a bestseller if ever there was one.

5:32. Kathy Mack says she's going to start referring to us as regulars. She serves us Cornish pasties filled with veal and beef, with a spinach salad on the side. I pick up the bill because Derek never re-fights a battle he previously lost. They must have taught him that in officer school.

7:01. Back on the street, we stop at a filling station just as it's closing. Derek convinces the attendant to fill up the tank before turning off the lights for the evening. They talk about basketball, specifically the World Professional Tournament that took place in Chicago a few months ago. Derek apparently knows a little something about every sport played in North America.

8:33. The sun officially sets over Kansas City.

8:49. We arrive at Family Investment Capital and park around back, as planned. Helena lets us in through a service entrance. She's dressed like Eleanor Roosevelt on a diplomatic mission to France. A table near the Telex machine serves as our headquarters. Helena dismissed her staff hours ago, and so the three of us sit undisturbed and talk about city politics, the heat, and reports of a new F-1 truck soon to be released by Ford. Derek is particularly eager to get a look at it, and Helena says something about men and their toys. Derek doesn't disagree.

9:16. Helena returns from the service door with Corky in tow. He has removed his tie and rolled up his sleeves. He's brought an unopened pack of cigarettes and a deck of cards. As bridge is a game designed for pairs play, he divides us up, and I end up sitting across from Derek, wondering if he's as keen at this game as he seems to be with so many others. Our opponents' strategy partly consists of obscuring our vision with smoke, as Corky is generous with his cigarettes, lighting another one for Helena every time she leans across the table.

9:52. We take turns checking 19th Street from the window, though we're hours too early. The lights are starting to go out at Club Mardi Gras across the street; it's a Tuesday, so business is slow. Back at the bridge table, king of spades wins, our trick. Derek and I sally forth and take an early lead, in spite of the smoke.

10:29. The conversation has turned to the war, and Helena asks Corky what rank he achieved. Corky tells her that he went in a private and came out a sergeant, though the only difference in the two was the amount of grief he had to bear from the officers. C-Rations tasted the same for everyone, regardless.

10:55. I need a break from the game because figuring out the optimal opening bid has always frustrated me. I excuse myself to use the ladies' room, glancing at the briefcase as I walk by, suddenly doubting my own plan. With my hands on the sink and eyes on the mirror, I pass all the judgments on myself and say all the Hail Marys, getting it all over with, tired of waiting around for absolution to come from someone else. I don't know why it's taken me this long.

11:02. I return to bridge and play with abandon. In the bathroom I decided to confront Gene Skinner because that's what you do with bravery when it comes your way. Now I try to decide the best time and place.

11:21. Derek and I win two out of three and take the match. He smiles across the table at me, and though I smile back, this moment is merely a cover story to conceal the truth. There's too much going on suddenly to put much emphasis on the results of a card game, so when I say thanks to Helena's congratulations on the victory, it feels like I'm giving an alias to avoid revealing the real me. We all spend the next twenty-seven minutes speaking of inane things.

11:48. "It's time," Corky says. We all rise from the table with its neatly stacked cards and messy ashtray, all else forgotten.

11:49. I take the briefcase by the handle.

11:50. Corky moves to a position near the corner of the window. Derek touches the gun in his pocket, just to make sure.

11:51. Helena kills the lights.

11:52. I open the door and step out into the summer air, Derek directly behind me, the stars overhead. They say that in bigger cities you can't see the night sky because of all the manmade lights. I hope that never happens here.

"Shall we?" Derek asks.

We walk to the curb and wait.

****

With the rare exception, I am always asleep by this time of day. I don't inhabit the world of the bartenders, the security guards, and the printers running off the morning edition of the *Star*. The stillness in the air surprises me. A dog barks in the distance. The buildings are little more than angular shadows, like flats on a stage with the house lights off.

The final minutes move by us in a manner I can almost feel. I stand in the darkness beside a man with a concealed gun, a container of stolen documents at my side. For the first time in my life, I am clandestine.

The sound of an approaching motor draws my attention from one gloomy end of the street to the other. It quickly grows louder as the vehicle nears.

"Inline eight-cylinder engine," Derek says, "two-hundred forty-eight cubic inches."

"You can tell that just by listening?"

"Tonto can discern the number of bandits by the sound of their horses' hooves."

"I see. Does that make me the Lone Ranger?"

"Oh, by now I've come to believe that all you lack is the mask."

That makes me smile, here in the dark.

Headlamps round the corner, causing me to squint as they sweep across my face. The black Buick Super rolls to a stop at the curb, and then the driver shuts off the engine, which ticks loudly in the otherwise quiet night.

Both doors swing open.

Not only is Derek beside me, but Corky watches from the window, only a few feet away. Both have killed other men and would probably not hesitate to do so again here tonight. What is almost unimaginable to me is reflex to them. The next few moments could play out in any number of ways.

"I always did appreciate punctuality," one of them

says, the driver, moving around the front of the car. He's in his shirtsleeves and suspenders, as the night is too hot for a coat. His partner wears a flat cap and smokes, but for the most part their features are impossible to discern.

I shift the case in front of me, holding the handle with both hands.

"You're Frisco, right?" the driver asks.

"Does that matter?"

"Where's your friend?"

"We have what you want."

"You talk to anyone about this?"

"No one knows but us."

"So you say." He jams his hands into his trouser pockets. By the ember of his partner's cigarette, I can barely see his eyes. "What about you, old chap?"

Derek doesn't move. I imagine his hand on the checkered grip of the Sauer. "I suggest you take what you came for and leave. No need to draw this out."

"Maybe we're not convinced you're going to keep your mouths shut."

"If that's the case, then the way I see it, you have two options."

"Yeah? And what are these options of mine?"

"One, you collect the ballots and leave, like your boss told you to. Or two, you take some liberties with the orders you've been given and tell us to get into your car to take a little ride."

"Number two sounds pretty interesting, now that you mention it."

Through this exchange, my heart behaves in the expected fashion, permitting me only the shallowest of breaths. Violent crime is not as uncommon here as it used to be, and they say it's only getting worse. Acting on that data, the FBI put one of its nine original field offices only a few miles away. Yet I stand without wavering—at least not visibly.

"You know the attorney for whom Mrs. Frisco here is working?" Derek asks.

"Sure, a fellow named Schneider. We did our homework. What of it?"

"Are you aware that Sergeant Schneider qualified as a marksman on the M1 Garand rifle?" Still without moving, Derek says to me, "Vivian, the Garand is chambered for what caliber, again?"

"Thirty-ought-six." I could load one of those shells while sleepwalking.

"Ah, right. Of course." To the men from the Buick, he says, "The good sergeant is positioned in the building directly behind us, and from this short distance, he could give you a third eye."

The men say nothing.

Now Derek leans in, only a little. "Do you want a third eye, *old chap*?"

I count the intervening seconds, a period in which everything teeters on a wire. It could fall either way, and I wouldn't know how I'd respond until instinct energized me like one of the switchboard plugs.

Very slowly the driver removes his hands from his pockets—empty. "All right. I hear you. Just pass the damn thing over."

I extend the briefcase, and the man with the cigarette snatches it from me.

"Little piece of advice," the driver says, moving around the car. "Climb out of the well before you drown. There ain't no bottom." He opens the car door. "That shit just keeps on going down."

Both doors slam. The big engine fires, the lights come on like glaring eyes, and they pull away into the street.

Chapter Thirty-Two

In Which I End a Friendship

Four shot glasses hold a combined six ounces, which is serendipitously the exact amount remaining in the bottle of single-malt whiskey Helena retrieves from the cabinet. Corky accepts the bottle and does the honor of pouring as we stand around the table with its scattered playing cards and mostly full ceramic ashtray. We've said little since the men drove away minutes ago. It's quarter after midnight as we each retrieve a glass.

Helena provides the toast: "May we never go to hell but always be on our way."

As one, we touch our glasses together, these ragtag musketeers and me, their would-be D'Artagnan, and then we toss the liquor down our throats.

****

As unlikely as it sounds to my own ears, it's nearly three a.m. when I close my door and lock it gently behind me. My friends and I released the tension of our illicit streetside exchange by laughing at one another's questionable jokes and telling mostly true stories of life before the war. Over the last few hours I did what I never do: indulge. Helena unearthed some Amontillado, and Corky produced another pack of cigarettes. We played a few rounds of poker, I lost my pile of leather buttons and old ration coupons we were using for wagers, and now—

seeking out my toothbrush and the warm bed beyond it—
I would like to call my night an epilogue but I know it's
not. As Robert Frost once wrote, I have promises to keep.

****

Yesterday, in the remains of the Dachau
Concentration Camp, four dozen members of the SS
were sentenced to death for war crimes. I read this in the
paper with my coffee and cereal bowl beside me.
Sunlight slants through the eastern windows. I turn the
page and check the box scores and schedule. Tomorrow
the Monarchs will host a home game against the New
York Cubans, with forty-year-old Satchel Paige taking
the mound. The sportswriter wonders if there's any
lightning left in the man's arm. I guess we'll see.

When my coffee's gone, I can delay no longer: I
need to call Betty and ask about Gene.

It's none of my business, some might say, except
these days I make everything my business, from boxing
matches to breaking and entering. Corky is my friend,
and more than that, I owe him. If there's something going
on behind his back, his former PI partner would have told
him, and so shall I.

I sit with the phone nearby, my hair unbrushed and
my feet bare.

*The best people in the world are the ones who don't
let go,* a boy once said to me.

I dial the switchboard and ask to be connected to the
home of Corky and Betty Schneider.

Folks sometimes ask me, upon learning where I
work, what happens to make the phone ring on the other
end. Do I transmit some kind of secret signal down the
line from the switchboard? Do I press a certain button? I
tell them it's simply an electric impulse that moves along

a wire and instructs the clapper to start rattling against the bell. There's no magic in that—and yet there is. In that uncertain time from the first ring until the receiver is picked up, all things are possible.

I consider this as I hold the phone against my ear and wait. At this time of the morning, Corky will be in the office or perhaps on his way to court on behalf of a client, and Betty will be doing those things that the Bettys of the world do. You see them in magazines.

"Schneider residence, this is Betty speaking."

"Hello, Betts."

"Vivian?"

I have planned nothing from this point forward. I let the words move through me in a way they wouldn't have two weeks ago. "I want to talk to you for a few minutes, if that's all right."

"Of course."

"I'm going to ask some questions."

"Sounds fun. Let me take a seat. I was in the middle of dusting that credenza we inherited from Corky's father and I don't at all mind the reprieve. That old thing is full of nooks and crannies. What *is* a cranny, anyway?"

"A tiny opening or narrow crack."

"How is that different from a nook?"

"A nook is a small space in a corner."

"How do you know that?"

"I spend a lot of time alone with crossword puzzles. Have you ever stayed at the Tuscany Lane Motor Court?"

Moments pass.

"It's out on Highway Fifty," I tell her. "Are you familiar with it?"

"Why, I suppose I am. I've lived in this city for years

now. What a peculiar question. Vivian, are you feeling well?"

"Do you know a man by the last name of Diantonio?"

"I'm not sure why you're asking me these things." Her voice has changed.

"Mr. Diantonio owns the motor court."

"Good for him. Are you going somewhere with this? I'm not entirely sure I appreciate it."

"Have you ever spent time in one of Mr. Diantonio's rented rooms?"

"Why is this any of your concern?"

"I'll take that as a yes."

"Vivian, stop this."

"Did you spend time in that room with Gene Skinner?"

"*Stop this now.*" She hangs up.

The line goes dead.

I return the receiver to its cradle, my heart not beating as quickly as I anticipated it might. Last night's meeting on the sidewalk was frightening enough that I suppose accusing my friend of adultery barely increases my pulse.

The phone rings, which doesn't surprise me at all. Have I moved entirely beyond surprises? I pick it up. "Hello, Betty."

"Goddamn you, Vivian."

"Are you going to tell Corky or shall I?"

Silence. She's probably startled by my response, the coldness of it, the way it sounds like some kind of exotic metal striking my teeth—cobalt, perhaps, something normally foreign to both of us. What I'm feeling is anger, anger mixed with sadness, and I am no longer docile enough to soften it or give it a less threatening name.

Then, almost in a whisper: "What do you want?" Her tone, like mine, is something neither of us has heard before.

"What I've always wanted. The truth."

"This has nothing to do with you."

"You'd rather me just pretend that nothing's wrong? I can't do that."

"Of course you can't, because these days you're the world-famous lady investigator who thinks she can help solve a homicide on account of her husband being a decent private eye when he was alive, and God forbid the rest of us just try minding our own business."

"You need to tell—"

"I don't need to do anything. Stay out of my life. Stay out of *everyone's* life. I'm sorry that you're sad and alone with nobody in your bed but your cat, but that doesn't give you this kind of right."

"What if I ask Mr. Diantonio at the motor court about you?"

"Ask Diantonio, ask David Niven, ask Harry Truman for all I care. See how far you get with all your questions. And Vivian, while you're at it…"

"Yes?"

"Go to hell."

She hangs up, this time for good.

I sip a second mug of coffee. The line about the cat was mean, but nothing I didn't deserve. I'm standing half-dressed at my window, gazing down at Nat Looper in the morning sunshine. He's reading a newspaper. The milk delivery truck stops at the corner. A man in white hops out, his bottles in a wire basket.

Derek will drive his fancy car away tomorrow. Part

of me wants to analyze my feelings about that, and perhaps there will be time for that later, but something Betty said is drumming its fingers in my mind. I'm not sure why. In her anger, she told me to take up the issue with President Truman and also David Niven. The famous actor seems to star in every war picture released in the cinemas these days, and now he's looking at me with those blue British eyes of his, trying to get my attention.

I leave the window and move slowly about the room, cup in hand, my gaze on nothing in particular. Just as slowly, I drift back to my reflection in the glass, closing in on something.

An autographed photograph of Niven stands on Corky's desk, opposite a picture of Betty. In my mind, I walk around the office, a place I have visited so often through the years that I can reconstruct it down to the dent in the corner of the filing cabinet. I run my finger along the back edge of the chair in which I usually sit, trying to bring everything with me at once: Betty's rage, Niven's blue eyes, Kaz's broom, and Corky's kindness when he squeezed my hand yesterday.

I bite my lip, my breath catching behind my teeth.

You inherited Jim's key, I said to him.

Still not breathing, I move in my mind from the office to the building's lobby and the exit door set into the rear wall. *This leads outside*, I told Helena.

Sure, she replied. *So there's parking out back?*

Yes, but this door isn't used by the public. It stays locked.

I'll say it again. I'm lost.

Whoever killed Kaz came in through this door. It's the only other way inside.

They picked the lock?
Or?

As the Helena of my memory says it, I let out my breath and repeat it with her in front of my living-room window: "Or they had a key."

Chapter Thirty-Three

In Which I Find My *Ikigai*

What I do next must be done with precision. I work it out as I pace, circumnavigating my small living room, moving from the sunlight of the window to the shadows of the bookshelf and back again. Shelved beside the Margaret Mitchell where I keep my earnings is a dictionary, and if I opened it up to the V section, this is what I might see:

vivian \ˈviv-ee-en\ (noun): one known for dogged perseverance in obtaining personal details that are not readily or publicly available; *also*: busybody.

The first of my four telephone calls is complete. Three remain. There's a certain symmetry in the fact that one of my primary tools in all of this is the phone. I spend my afternoons connecting folks across the country and sometimes the world. And so here I am again, hoping for a few final connections that will bring everything home.

Corky answers his office line in a rush. When he hears my voice, he says he has a million and one things to do, so maybe I can give him a shout after lunch.

"I just need a moment."

"Make it a quick one."

I feel instantly as if I'm deceiving him, because even as we speak, his life may be headed toward a precipice of my own creation. "I'm hoping you can tell me something."

"After last night, what more could you possibly need?"

"Information."

"Viv, I'm due in court in less than an hour—"

"Where do you keep the second key?"

"Come again?"

"Jim's key to the building. Where is it?"

"In a shoebox of random knickknacks on my bureau at home. Why?"

"Does Betty know it's there?"

I can hear his not-quite silent frustration at my questions. "Of course she does. She dusts the house like a woman possessed. What are you driving at?"

"I'll let you know soon. In the meantime, talk to your wife. And one more thing."

"Yeah?"

"I'm sorry." I hang up before he can ask why.

****

Alexander Graham Bell didn't invent the telephone. His patents built on the work of others who produced functioning prototypes years earlier. Ms. Peele told me that, disabusing me of the lessons I was taught in school. I can imagine her now, standing behind the stool where I'm scheduled to sit this afternoon, wondering what's going on.

Call number three: Gene Skinner, aka Eugene.

Back on the couch with the pearl-colored receiver against my ear, I wait for his workplace phone to ring. Gene parleyed his experience in an army communications office into writing copy for print advertisements. He works in a trendy building on the Missouri side of the city, the kind of place where they redecorate every season according to what's supposedly fashionable in New York. I'm told it's currently wallpapers of contrasting hues.

The phone rings.

My thoughts are not as messy as the notes I'm keeping on my stenographer's pad; everything is aligning itself—keys, brooms, motor court trysts. When the truth begins to emerge from these pieces, it doesn't frighten me as it might have two weeks ago. I accept it with that same metallic hardness that I felt moments ago toward Betty.

The phone rings.

I've not prepared anything to say. Eleven days ago, I nervously scripted every question I posed to Wallace Breckenridge, afraid of omitting an important detail or revealing the extent of my uncertainty. But that time is gone. I'm no longer wearing yesterday's life.

The line is picked up. A second passes.

Then: "Kanter Company, how may I help you today?"

"Is Mr. Skinner available, please?"

"Yeah, sure. Hold the line."

That is something I've recently learned to do quite well. *Hold the line.*

The line crackles distantly: "Skinner here."

"Gene, it's Vivian."

"I'm sorry, did you say—"

"I spoke with Betty this morning."

"Vivian?"

I've never called him before, at work or anywhere else, so the confusion in his voice is honest. "Yes, that's right. I think you and I should talk."

"All right. Talk about what?"

"I know about the broom."

Gene says nothing at all.

"There's an empty warehouse out on the river. Meet me there in one hour." I give him the address and hang up without saying goodbye.

****

My fourth and final call was to Derek, of course, and now I find myself in my V-8 chariot, the top down and the sun on my face. I've given him the details, but it's too loud to talk, between the engine and the wind. By now the Schneider house might be falling apart.

I push that aside and watch the city give way to the wilderness. The road runs along the river's edge. Boys play on the muddy bank, two of them with poles in the water, the rest splashing sufficiently that no fish will likely come near. I learned to swim in that river, not far from this very spot.

Gene's car is already here when we ease to a stop among the weeds in the shadow of the building. He leans against the Packard's fender, smoking, his sleeves rolled up and his hat protecting his eyes.

Derek turns off the engine. "You sure about this?"

"I'm not sure about anything anymore."

"Why bring him here?"

"So he can see."

"See what?"

My only reply is to swing open the door and climb from the car.

Derek does the same. He wears his sport coat despite the heat because the coat has a pocket and the pocket has a gun.

Gene lifts his weight off the fender as we approach, straightening to his full height, giving a slight roll of his neck. He's always been athletic, running around the streets at sunrise and drawing puzzled glances from his neighbors.

I don't stop, just walk toward the warehouse, doing my best to ignore the force of my heart against my ribs. I reach the door through which I have passed twice before, once as an interloper among the refugees and the second time as the reason they had to flee. I open the door, then bend down carefully and remove my shoes, as I was asked to do when this place was someone's home. I look back at Gene, who is staring at me. I lied when I told him that I knew about the broom. That was just a hunch. But by the sharp angle of his eyes, I know it's true.

I step inside, and after a moment he follows.

****

Months from now, this building will be overrun with birds that have entered through the broken skylights. Unless someone takes an interest and invests in upkeep, grass will push up through the cracked floor. I walk to the square table in the middle of the vast space. Upon it rests the book that I placed here three days ago and the origami owl that someone left behind. Though I'll never know for sure, I sense that Jesse Imada placed this here as some kind of talisman, a ward against the evil he was fleeing. I pick it up and place it in my palm where Gene Skinner can see it.

"What are we doing out here?" Gene stands about ten feet from the doorway in his polished black business shoes. He shoots a glance over his shoulder at Derek, then back at me. "Seriously, Vivian, what the hell?"

"Kazuhiko Agawa was trying to help the people who made their home in this place."

"I've never been here in my life."

"I believe you. Kaz wasn't killed because he was aiding people in need or even because he was Japanese."

Gene crosses his arms. Every tiny muscle in his jaw is visible.

I try to hold the owl steady, but my hand trembles. "At some point I realized there was no broom."

"I don't know what you're talking about."

"When Helena Crenshaw and I stopped by Corky's office, I looked in the broom closet. I saw a mop, a bucket, and plenty of rags. But no broom."

"Your point?"

"The broom handle was used to hit Kaz in the head. After he fell, I suppose he was punched or kicked to death."

Gene doesn't move. He is, in fact, unnaturally still.

"My guess is that the broom ended up in the river."

Finally, slowly, he shakes his head. "I'm leaving." He turns toward the door—

"Kazuhiko Agawa accidentally interrupted you and Betty while you were being indiscreet in her husband's office."

That stops him.

"To convince him to keep his mouth shut, you used the second key to enter the rear lobby door and confront him."

Gene twists around to face me again.

I keep holding the owl that jitters on my palm, like it will somehow protect me, like it might help me transfer the guilt to where it belongs. "Anger and bigotry got the better of you, and you struck him with his own broom. After that, you couldn't stop yourself. Maybe he said something that sent you over the edge."

"Yeah? You don't know shit."

"If I asked your wife where you were in the early morning hours of July second, would she say you were at home?"

He moves his hands down to his sides and makes two fists. "Sounds like you're just inventing wild stories and hoping I take the bait."

"What about Betty?"

"What about her?"

"I'm not sure how much she knows about all of this. Maybe after getting caught with you, she suspects what happened to Kaz. Or maybe you told her everything that transpired after that. Either way, I wouldn't expect her to hold up very well under questioning."

From somewhere outside comes the sound of the wind rushing through riverside branches. The gust rattles the sheet-metal roof. Inside, though, nothing moves. Derek stands in the doorway, my new and cherished friend, my driver, my confidant. Between us, Gene is like a figure cast in stone, trim and muscled, his face defiant. The moments pass among us with no witnesses but the owl.

I've never seen a switchblade outside of the movies. A four-inch blade appears in Gene's hand as if by legerdemain, summoned instantly without any movement at all. There is only the sound in the silence, a reptilian *snick*, a wink of light off steel.

Gene lunges toward me.

He is athletic, and I am trapped in a paralysis of my own making. I understand in that second that he intends to seize me, put that blade against me, and then march me past Derek into whatever violent world waits outside. Yet all I can do is to begin to close my eyes—I have become many new things in recent days, but a warrior is not one of them.

Derek fires a bullet into the table.

Gene skids to a stop, the crack of the gunshot echoing hard off the walls. I let out a sound and stagger backward, nearly falling. Derek shifts the barrel so that it's pointed at Gene's face. I get my legs beneath me and lock my knees in place before I tumble, the paper owl scrunched between my fingers.

For the longest time, no one moves. The round from the Sauer drilled a hole in the table only a few feet away from where I stand. My eyes dart wildly. Derek keeps his arm extended. It feels as if either of the men could suddenly burst, so delicately are we all balanced. My instinct is to seek cover, but I'm held in place by whatever force is holding the moment intact. For some reason I remember dropping a nickel in Nat Looper's cup, hoping it would grant us luck. From there, the days advance like a film reel in my mind, and I see all the faces I've encountered, good and bad.

At some point, the knife clatters to the floor.

Epilogue

In Which I Sit Behind Home Plate

That afternoon, the Kansas City Monarchs host the New York Cubans, and Derek has brought me to the game. We didn't arrive until midway through the second inning, having spent several hours with the police, but now the sun is shining down on none other than Satchel Paige as he goes up oh-and-two on a batter in the top of the fourth.

Derek crunches a peanut shell in his fingers and pops one into his mouth. "You know I hit the road tomorrow. My leave officially ends."

I'm trying not to think about that. The Monarchs are already up by three.

He cracks open another nut. "I was, um… I was wondering if it might be acceptable to give you a call later this week. I'm curious to know how all of this plays out—with the Schneiders and the police and everything."

I turn my head slightly and glance at him from under the brim of my hat. "I don't suppose you'd consider leaving your car behind, would you?"

He smiles. "Something tells me the next time we meet, you'll be driving one of your own."

"Stranger things have happened. But I won't be driving it to the switchboard."

"You're thinking about quitting?"

"I'm thinking I've been fired."

"You didn't call in this afternoon? You just... skipped?"

"The least of my multiple transgressions, all things considered."

"A fair point."

We return our divided attention to the game. The infielders are bantering back and forth. The umpire pauses the game to wipe the sweat from his face. The Cubans' dugout hollers encouragement to the batter, while the man on the mound makes the ball do things in the air beyond the ken of any white player in the majors.

"So what next?" Derek asks.

What next, indeed? I don't quite have an answer, but in the last few days I've gained momentum, the first forward motion I've experienced since Jim went to war and never came home. Something that once seemed impossible—escaping the grief—now feels delicately real. "I think it's time I found new employment."

"I'm sure Corky could be persuaded to bring you aboard full-time as a legal assistant."

"Maybe. But do you think he'd rather have an in-house investigator?"

"A detective on retainer?"

"Like I said, stranger things have happened."

He smiles. We watch the next two pitches in silence.

"I mentioned calling you later this week," he says.

"So you did."

"You don't think the women at the switchboard will gossip or anything when they connect me to your line? I wouldn't want to cause any trouble."

"I think it's a little late for that. You are officially

guilty of aiding and abetting a known troublemaker. But if it makes you feel any better, I can tell you how to dial me directly."

"What? That's possible?"

"A secret of the trade." I look away from the game long enough to find his eyes. "You wouldn't consider that improper, would you? Dialing me direct?"

He lets a few seconds pass before saying, "No, ma'am, I would not."

A warmth passes through me, a kind of heat I've not felt in a long time. "I look forward to it. But"—I let out an overdue sigh—"I need to have one more important telephone conversation before then."

"Mrs. Agawa?"

"Yes."

"She'll be happy to hear from you."

"I'm not sure about the happy part, but at least she'll finally know."

"I suspect you'll be locally famous by this time tomorrow, once the newspapers hear."

"You think?"

"Oh, the reporters are probably all ringing you at this very moment, now that the police report has been filed. A few are probably standing around your door, just waiting. You want to leave and head back home to chat with them?"

I know he's kidding me. I smile at him—authentically, simply, and without expectation.

He smiles back. "I didn't think so."

Pure daylight shines down on us, Mr. Paige hurls a meteorite at the batter, and I accept a peanut from the handsome man beside me.

My name is Vivian Frisco, and this is my town.

A word about the author…

Dr. Lance Hawvermale published his first books under the female pseudonym of Erin O'Rourke. Since then, his poetry and fiction have garnered numerous awards.

Hawvermale is an alumnus of AmeriCorps, performing his service on the Otoe-Missouria tribal lands in Red Rock, Oklahoma. He has worked as a college dean, an editor, and a youth counselor. He lives in Texas with his family and their honey bees.

Visit his website at www.lancehawvermale.com http://www.lancehawvermae.com

Thank you for purchasing
this publication of The Wild Rose Press, Inc.

For questions or more information
contact us at
info@thewildrosepress.com.

The Wild Rose Press, Inc.
www.thewildrosepress.com

www.ingramcontent.com/pod-product-compliance
Lightning Source LLC
Chambersburg PA
CBHW052021020726

47501CB00004B/1166